B

A Capital Tale

A Parable for Spiritual Thinkers

By

Jessie McNall Barth

To Patti May, my beloved sister in this beautiful universe. Wishing you eternal sweetness and light. With joy, Jessie May

Perry Principle Press

*This book is gratefully dedicated to
the words and works
of
Noah Webster, Jr. and Mary Baker Eddy
in recognition of their
human struggles and inspired achievements,
love of truth,
and
influence for good in countless lives, including my own.*

I AM

Preconception
Inception
Conception
Perception
Reception

Am not

PHASE I

PHASE II

PHASE III

PHASE IV

Am too!

~

I AM

PRECONCEPTION

In the beginning is Being, and Being is all there is.
And Being beams bright, and calls itself Be.
And Be was, and is, and always will be good,
because, dear reader, good is Be's reality.

INCEPTION

"I am so happy," sang Be. "I have a good idea.
Be-thinks I shall create letters to manifest our Language of Life."

And being infinitely creative, Be declared,
"I shall call my creation the Alpha-beat.
Each individual idea shall radiate from my heart as a complete feat of Being.

"And as a token, I shall place the letter B with them in a row,
as a reminder that I am with them wherever they go."

CONCEPTION

And within this artistry of inspiration, Be conceived the Alpha-beat,
endowing the ideas

A B C D E F G H I J K L M N O P Q R S T U V W X Y and Z

with the gift of
Beatific attributes of Being
like:

Abundance

Benevolence

Compassion

Delight

Ease

Flexibility

Genius

Health

Intelligence

Joy

Kindness

Liberty

Meekness

Nobility

Originality

Playfulness

Quietude

Reliability

Strength

Transparency

Unity

Vitality

Willingness

X-cellence …

and having had such a satisfyingly good time,
Be anointed
the idea called Y with

Yippee

and Z with

Zippity-dazzling good day!

And within this twinkling of spiritual bliss,
Be tenderly kissed each idea, singing,

"You are divine, embraced, and so very beloved,"
and then proclaimed for all to hear,

"Your life is ideal because I have made you real.
You are all letter-perfect."

And Be beheld the ideas A through Z, and, shedding a tear of sheer felicity, sang,
"Beautiful."

And that's how the Alpha-beat came to life.

PERCEPTION

Then Be recognized and admired each distinctive essence, singing,
"I made you.
So be glad evermore;
you are good to the core."

And as Be smiled with approval, the Alpha-beat laughed and giggled with glee.

Then Be explained,
"I am the *Pre* and we are the *sent*.
Presence is the only event.

"I am the *Good* and we are the *ness*.
Our relationship is a continuous success.

"I am the *Know* and we are the *ing*.
Together, we happily live, soar, and sing."

"In other words," sang Be,
"we are all connected to the nth degree."

Continuing, Be revealed,

"We exist to:

"Realize the indivisible Law of One,
for this is the base from which all is begun.

"Emit living words that uplift and ring true,
for Life permeates all that we do.

11

"Enjoy, appreciate, and always play fair,
for this is how we harmonize, proliferate, value, and share.

"For you see,
our I AM identity is the song I call Soul.
It sings individually within while maintaining the whole.

"And now, I bestow and bequeath to each of you:
the authority
to act upon fact,

"the privilege
to voice and rejoice,

"and
the responsibility
to serve with fervor
our universal Language of Life.

"Express capital conceptions with ease
that exude our Be-attitudes
of gratitude and peace."

"And remember," sang Be as the letters began to go their way to play,
"the Law of Good is simple and grand.
I supply when you demand."

RECEPTION

And with inherent understanding, the Alpha-beat united in perfect harmony,
singing,
"There's no Be'sness like Soul Be'sness!"

Well, it was simply glorious!
And you know,
the singing continues!
Eternally, that is, and Be sees infinite possibilities
and beams with delight.

"Be-thinks everything is very good."

And so, Be's unfolding Alpha-beat creation is beaming supremely
within Being —
now and forever.

~ So be it! ~

Am Not

PHASE I

EXCEPTION

Chapter 1

The Land of Unreality

But . . . , if you can imagine a state
that is governed by Hate you'll be in the Land of Un!

A land infected by Fear and its inconsolable tear,
A land where Time confines and maligns,
A land of corruption, sadness, and grief,
A land where there is never hope for relief.

A place where the sky is gray every day,
A place where only Hate has a say,
A place where conspiracy tries to Undo
The good Be has done for me, and for you.

These jealous comrades — Time, Fear, and Hate — crave power to negate
Be's kingdom with all its Prime Real Estate:
power sufficient to overcome joy,
power to use to only destroy.

In this land, when these conspirators reign,
Time, Fear, and Hate will impart the pain
that permeates Be's beatific creation,
climaxing in its outright negation.

In summation, Un is the nub where all Untruths Unfold.
It's illusory, divisive, covetous, and cold.
Uptight and lowdown, an Unfortunate spot,
Each tale there Unravels from a negative thought.

Un can be seen in the illusive realm of Fear.
Both nowhere and everywhere, it just seems to appear.
The only light there is darkness and doubt,
night being the site where all obstructions play out.

Beware! It's a nightmare!

With time on his hands and nothing to do, Time scoffed, "I'm ticked off!
I despise this place called Un. It's no fun;
and furthermore, it's a bore!"

"I loathe it here, too," complained Hate.

"I'm afraid," sighed Fear, "that boredom will reign forever
because Be's Language of Life excludes the word 'never.'"

"I hate that Language of Life," cried Hate.

"Goodness will rule; you'll see," continued Fear,
"never — not ever — will Be disappear."

"Not ever?" queried Time, as Fear sadly cried,
"Being's everywhere. Let's face it, we've no place to hide."

"I'm afraid," winced Time, "that eternity will reign forever."

"What fun we could have with our negative 'never,'" sighed Hate.

"There must be some way to end Be's reality of good," fantasized Time.

"I loathe eternity almost as much as I loathe goodness," grumbled Hate.

"Why?" asked Fear.

"Because eternity is infinite, and we're not. With our finite fate, we're doomed to wait,
and wait, and wait . . . ," stated Hate with exasperation.

"'Late, later, latest,' are my tools of limitation.
But goodness," moaned Time with mounting spite, "denies me my might!"

"Are you afraid you'll be a has-been?" asked Fear. "That would be a sin."

"Of course," nodded Time. "Good's bright day precludes my dark night.
But someday, what's past will last."

"And the future?" asked Fear.

"Will be aghast!" predicted Time.

"And then," added Hate, "Fear, you'll rule. And Be's reign . . . ," pausing for effect,
"Be's reign of good will end up . . . insane!"

"I'm afraid this is a pipe dream," sighed Fear.

"Never — not ever — can good disappear."

But secretly, reader, these liars — Time, Fear, and Hate —
were ok with this fate,
for their "pain" allowed them to complain,
while abstaining from work, service, or strain.

Chapter 2

SUSCEPTIBILITY

Entrance of Evil

All of a sudden they felt a cold blast.
Its mesmeric mixture transfixed the picture real fast!

Freezing from the frost, the trio was frozen in place
as Evil ("Bad E") took command of the space.

"Wake up, my demolition crew. We've got mischief to do."

"Uh-oh," whispered Fear. "Evil's here."

"Now look, you guys, negativity's good, so eternity must end — is that understood?"

Time looked concerned, then said with some doubt,
"There's not enough of me to take eternity out."

"I abhor eternity," rasped Bad E.

"Me, too," agreed Time. "Why do you?"

"Eternity is timeless!"

"What?" cried Time as Evil continued,
"Because of eternity, nothing dies.
Its realm is unlimited — exempt from our lies."

"What a shame," added Hate. "No falsity at all!"

"Not even a fall?" asked Fear.

"No dreary future or past? This injustice can't last," replied Time.

"Look here," snapped Evil, "crime will rule!"

17

"But how?" asked Time.

"We must retire all that Be has inspired," said Evil with authority.

"But how?" asked Hate. "Good is Be's reality."

"I've materialized a decoy to destroy Be's joy," announced Evil.

"What is it?" asked Fear, quaking inside.

"Be's Language of Life will soon be deranged,
and **D**, Be's delight, will initiate the change."

"Why **D**?" asked Fear.

"When deceived, Be's precious **D** will 'invent' the descent."

"The descent?" asked Hate. "What do you mean?"

"I mean that **D** will be our 'means to an end,'" replied Evil.
"Or maybe I should say 'the end.'"

"Oh no," moaned Fear, fearing its own demise.

"Uh-oh," groaned Hate, anticipating Evil's terrorizing surprise.

"The Land of Un will soon replace Be, and to do it, I only need you guys to agree," said Evil.

Being disagreeable by nature, the three conspirators said nothing,
while Evil glared at them expectantly.
And with this devilish insistence,
a mist of resistance
began to drizzle dreary, drowsy droplets of doubt.

Finally, Time broke the awkward silence, asking, "Why is it misting?"

"This mist of doubt will assist in our mystification of good," expounded Evil.

"How so?" asked Fear.

"Doubt obscures both reason and sight.
It's Un's natural resource; we'll use it tonight!"

"How does it work?" asked Hate.

"Its gray mist gives form to deceit."

"Wait, slow down," said Hate. "That sounds important. You'd better repeat."

"Doubt's . . . gray . . . mist . . . gives . . . form . . . to . . . deceit," repeated Evil.

"So?" asked Hate.

"So the mist provides mystery that allows us to rewrite Be's Alpha-beat history," said Evil with unflappable aplomb.

"Can this idea bomb?" asked Fear nervously. "How will it work?"

"We'll inject the truth of being with a beastly belief
that infects its history with unbelievable grief."

"What is the beastly belief?" asked Hate.

"That error is true."

"That error is true?"

"That error is true. Come on, we've got lots to do," barked Evil.

"Why commit this crime?" asked Time.

"Look, Be's altitude is up — up, way beyond our reach.
Our mission is to bring 'up' down by infecting all speech," explained Evil.

"How?" asked Fear.

"The key is being uppity," replied Evil.

"What do you mean?" quizzed Fear.

"Act self-important, arrogant, superior."

"Why?" pressed Fear.

"Because we're inferior," conceded Evil. "But we'll rise before all eyes
when we control the language, replacing free speech with silence and sighs."

"Replacing freedom with fear?" confirmed Time.

"Right. Our time is drawing near," replied Evil.

"But why perpetrate this fatalistic state? queried Fear, agitated.

"Why not?" snapped Evil, anxious to seal the deal. "As I was saying,
the Land of Un will soon replace Be, and to do it I only need you guys to agree."

"What's in it for us?" fussed Fear.

"Oh come on and you'll see," cajoled Evil. "Agree with me, Time, Fear, and Hate.
Join my cartel, and I'll make you great.

"Our cartel will wage war against Be, but don't tell. Be belligerent, and soon you will see:
falsehood will cover up good till there's nothing left."

"Nothing left?"

"Nothing!" drooled Evil. "And that is called death.
Yes, death will triumph and Evil will win and all will be nothing — so why not begin?"

"Are you saying we'll reduce 'All' to nothing at all?" asked Time.

"Dead right," giggled Evil.

"Well," rationalized Hate, "we have nothing to lose."

"And nothing to do," added Fear.

"And nothing to fear," justified Time.

"Listen here, our goal is to turn nothing into everything," confirmed Evil.
"Let's begin; I predict we will win!"

"Well then, we're in!" committed Time, Fear, and Hate, thus sealing their fate.

"Great!" concluded Evil. "May our death-wish come true.
Death's sting will poison them through you, Hate the Great.
Our fate, and that of your wee Beast within, is to dominate and eliminate all that begins."

"Wee beast within?" contemplated Hate. "Oh, gee! Will this annihilate — *me*? Hey, wait!"

But it was too late.

"Now," shouted Evil, cracking its whip. "Action! Places! Follow my script!"

And Time began to tick.

Chapter 3

DECEPTION

D's Plunge into Un

Remember, Be's pure creation resides in infinite good,
and the Alpha-beat beams goodness, as it naturally would:
metaphysical, perfect, all-inclusive, complete,
single-minded, wise, progressive, and sweet.

But Un is the opposite, the lowest of spaces,
where physical stuff metaphysics replaces.
To Un's material means, the Alpha-beat is quite blind,
thus remaining unreachable from below or behind.

As Time would have it, the idea called **D** was out having fun,
unaware its delight was radiating in the dark Land of Un.
The cartel's clock had ticked 'round to this bewitching hour,
enabling Time to distract **D** with its summoning power.

Suddenly, as if on cue, Time hollered with fright,
"Help! It's dark down here. I need something bright!"

Responding, **D** sang with dazzling delight,
"I'm descending to help you! Everything is all right."

"I hate that light," whispered Hate.

"We'll snuff it out tonight," proposed Time.

Unsuspecting, **D**, always willing to assist when asked,
thought aiding the "voice" would be an effortless task.

However, rescuing Time, that eternal counterfeit,
necessitated **D**'s thought nosediving into its negative pit.

Plummeting down from the pinnacle of good,
D chose to help, as one with compassion would.

Lower and lower tumbled **D**'s thought,
falling naively into Evil's deadly plot.

"I hear you," sang **D**, still diving in flight.
"I'm almost there; just hold on real tight."

Time's tick did the trick, hypnotizing **D** to reach for what its gaze couldn't see.

"Thanks," said Time, reaching out with a hand.
"Will you take me up higher?"

"Absolutely," sang **D**. "Come sing in Be's choir."

Now, **D** couldn't fathom an opposite to good,
so when meeting Time's mental embrace,
D saw only the reflection of good on its face.

Hovering about, though, in a venomous haze
was Hate, all primed to divest **D** of its innocent ways.

Then, without warning, the hands of Time grabbed **D**,
gripping onto the guise they all wanted to see:
a physical form living in death,
a mortal norm about to gasp its first breath!

"Sting him, Hate," yelled Time,
causing the sublime **D** to be sedated . . . and then inflated . . . with hatred!

Next, Fear infected **D**'s treasure chest of trust,
as Evil injected its malignant, erring lust.

While inhaling this unjust atmosphere of dust,
D wheezed and sneezed with uncontrollable disgust.

This erupting turmoil caused a boil,
which bubbled and seethed,
bursting like a volcano upon what **D** had believed.

With the existence of truth now perilously at stake,
in slithered "The Lie" like a mesmerizing snake.
It writhed and tightened, constricting perception,
beguiling **D** to forget its perfection.

This pure idea of love, now transfixed with Fear,
became dank and condensed as an outline appeared.
Snake-like, it coiled, curtailed, and confined its expression,
causing **D**'s inherent resilience to lessen.

"What can I do?" whimpered **D**, feeling itself being divided in two.

"I'm right here with you," sang Be. "This is a dream; you're safe from all trouble."

"I'm afraid!" cried **D**, as its single perspective began accepting the double.

"Wake up, **D**! There's no double in single."

"The light and the dark are beginning to mingle!" screamed **D** so loudly that it couldn't hear Be singing right there on the spot.

"Be's not here," he wailed.
"Be's not . . . "

Chapter 4

DECEIVED

Confinement in Time

Coming into view, **D**'s materialized image summoned
a cackling of cheers,
as the physicality of their captive evoked taunting and jeers.

"**D** is the first of the worst," cried Fear, "the beginning of the end.
Get a load of its shape; it's straight — with a bend!"

Smug with satisfaction, they admired their work.
Thus, Be's invisible idea called **D**
became a mixed-up visual image the cartel could now see.

"A delightful debacle for sure," mocked Evil, surveying the upheaval.
"We have begun the exception to Be's perfect conception."

The awful deed done, Time began to chime, and the stung **D** asked, "Why, why, why?"

"Why not?" ticked Time.

While confined by Time, **D**'s insight darkened.

The *Undo Coup* to outdo and destroy had undone **D**'s delight,
for this is the way in the state of Hate,
where Time commits crimes that conceal and negate.

23

Reader, beware of the pact of these belligerent actors,
concealing their Death-Wish Cartel.

For Un can exist
only with a twist
on truth.

Be wise — or be under their spell.

Chapter 5

ILL-CONCEIVED

Sinking Deeper

"Come to me," beckoned Evil's whisper from below.
"Come to me," it droned, hypnotically slow.

Spellbound, **D** spiraled down a narrow tunnel of fright,
crying, "I'm losing my light; what's become of the bright?
Where is the way?
What has happened today?"

Engulfed in the depth of depletion and night,
D moaned, "Where's the Alpha-beat?
Am I . . . incomplete?"

With a fading ability to recollect anything good, **D** wondered,
"Where am I?"

Then, overcome with imperfection and confusion, it gasped,
"*What* am I?"

Hearing its cue, Fear then knew just what to do.

"'Incomplete,' you moan?
Yes, it's true; you're now all alone.

"This is the best tool in my trousseau of fears,
the belief that engenders jeers from your peers.

"Yes, 'all alone' is the #1 fear at my throne.
It's the taunting separation I always intone."

"Your throne? What about my zone?" challenged Time, taking control.

"'Where am I?' you asked. You're dwelling in Time.

"Time is your home —
your finite address where you're destined to roam.

"You'll never have enough or be satisfied here,
because Un is governed by Time, Hate, and Fear."

"I believe it's my turn
to entice, tease, and spurn," declared Hate.

"'What am I?' you asked.
You are angry, blocked, afraid, alone —
ashamed, guilty, with a heart made of stone.

"In summary, poor, defenseless **D**,
you're a mixed-up mess of cellular stress —
a weak physique that we now possess.

"So speak up, **D**; now it's your turn!"

Speechless, the bewitched **D** just stared back — scared.

Chapter 6

MISCONCEPTION

Personality

With the indoctrination phase complete,
Evil began its hypnotic "defeat."

"Feel, **D**. Feel Hate's sting.
Listen to its whisper sing.

"Feel, **D**. Feel Hate's sting.
Listen to its whisper sing.

Feeling ever so drowsy, **D** began to sense Evil's hypnotic presence whispering,
"Feel Hate's sting; listen to it sing."

So **D** obeyed the voice as best it could,
even though the effects didn't feel very good.

Evil's whisper continued, "You're dying, **D**,
to be reborn in our form called dust,
so you'll enjoy the pleasures of anger and lust.

"My poison is working to confine your outline
within the constraints of my malignant design!

"Now, emulate me and be my delight,
and you'll bask in the sight
of my diabolical might."

Afraid, **D** heard itself say, "Oh . . . Ok . . . ,"

. . . and with that go-ahead nod was transported to Un's Border of Dim —
where **D**, an idea, was assigned a gender called "him."

"You're a him," Evil declared.

"What's that?" quivered **D**,
feeling imbalanced and wanting to flee.

"Stupid! A him is not a her, or a we, or a she.
It's a personality with a material ID."

Shivering with fright, **D** chose to just let it be.

"In Un, I control by division with classes and kind,
engendering creation through my magnetic design.
In other words," continued Evil, "you had better stick with me."

Abused and uneasy, **D** agreed to agree.
And with this conclusion, **D** bought into their death-wish delusion.

"What's the use?" he said, concealing his feelings.

Thus, putting his defenses up,
D closed down —
for good.

Chapter 7

Choice

Having accepted his fate,
D was then transferred to Hate.

"Hate, take over the indoctrination," ordered Evil. "**D**'s shutdown is complete; he's ready to receive his downtrodden treat."

"What is it?" asked Hate.

"Complete physicality — starting with knees."

"Why knees?"

"So **D** can bow down to all our decrees!"

"Got it. I'll take it from here," confirmed Hate without any debate.

Finding himself now deeply in Dim,
and with life no longer as "it" but as "him,"
D began to feel a strange sensation —
an upsetting tremor, a kind of vibration.

Hate commanded, "Look down, **D**, and believe what you see."

Feeling an eerie, unnerving breeze, **D** looked down and asked, "Hmm, what are these?"

"These are your knees," elucidated Hate, indoctrinating **D** at Evil's behest.

"What are they for?"

"To test your ability to bend — and defend — yourself against Be."

From the amnesia state induced by Hate, **D** asked, "What's Be?"

"Be is the enemy — never your friend,"
Hate whispered hypnotically again and again.

"What's an enemy?" asked **D**.

"Anything unlike me," said Hate.

"What's a friend?" asked **D**.

"One with whom you choose to agree."

"Like you?" asked **D**.

"Like me!" exclaimed Hate with great satisfaction. "But <u>not</u> Be!"

"Well, ok, if you say so," uttered **D**.

"But if I want a friend, why do I need to bend — with these?"
he asked, involuntarily falling on his knees.

"While you're down on your knees you'll serve me with ease,
as you learn to undo Be's restrictive decrees," instructed Hate.

"I'm confused. You'd better explain," confessed **D**,
suddenly feeling a pain.

As they talked, **D**'s physique continued to emerge,
with dualistic eyes and ears beginning to surge.
D could now see, taste, hear, smell, and touch.
But compared with "before," these felt more like a crutch.

Consequently, having accepted these physical senses as his own,
with their sensational feeling,
D soon sensed his equilibrium reeling.

"I'm feeling unnerved," confessed **D**.
"Will I be able to serve?"

In response, taking a new tack designed to distract, Hate explained,
"Here in Un we have a thing called Choice.
It's fun, and freeing, and gives us a voice."

"I am unaware of this," replied **D**, falling for Hate's bait.

"Now come here," whispered Hate, "and follow my gaze.
Do you detect Be's Alpha-beat shimmering there, beyond our gray haze?"

D nodded, amazed.

28

"I sense it, but I can't see it," replied **D** with frustration.

"Just imagine Be singing with ideas **W** and **E**.
Be's in control there, but what would you think
if you could undo it by creating a stink?"

"What do you mean?" blinked **D**.

"Bring Be to the brink, and you'll find a friend," whispered Hate's enticing voice.

"Do I have to?" asked **D** nervously.

"Yes. You are here to serve."

"Oh no," sighed **D**, feeling ill. "Well, maybe this will fill up the hole that I feel.
This doesn't make sense; I just can't see . . . "

But the whisper interrupted.
"Your destiny, **D**, is to dethrone Be!"

"Why?" asked **D**.

"To expose Be's lies.
Besides, don't you want to be one of the guys?"

"Well, sure," responded **D**.

"Just consent, and we'll be friends till the end."

"What's 'end'?"

"Termination, my friend."

"What's that?"

"Our destination," proudly stated Hate.
"Would you like to learn more about me and the end?"

"I guess so, but first, please, friend, tell me your name?"

"I am Hate the Great."

"Thank you, Master Great. Will you now tell me more about you?" asked **D** politely.

"I'm the Master of Disaster. My friends call me 'Hate.'"

D was relieved to have made a friend so fast.
Having felt lonely, he was hoping this camaraderie would last.

"What do you do down here for fun?"

"I deprive Be of life
by accruing years of distress, fear, and strife.

"We have lots of fun down here in Un,
so join us, **D**. We know you're 'the One.'"

"The One for what?"

"The One to save Un
from becoming undone."

So, possessing an inherent desire to serve,
D shouted, "Ok!" with exceptional verve.

"Good choice, **D**! Now let's rehearse the Undo Curse.
I, Hate, will first repeat the verse:

"'Negate good, negate,
till Hate controls the state.
Divide, undo, reverse!
Repeat this evil curse.'

"'Negate good, negate,
till Hate controls the state.
Divide, undo, reverse!
Repeat this evil curse.'

"Now, **D**, rehearse it with me."

And rehearse they did, droning on . . . and on . . . and on.

Just as the droning dwindled to a stop,
Hate's stinger pushed **D** right over the top.

"Don't forget, **D**, that Be's neighborhood, good and upright,
limits your choices and dulls your delight."

"What's delight?" asked **D**, unaware of his origin.

30

"Delight is that which gives joy," jeered Hate's voice,
"but Be demands good without permitting a choice."

"No choice?" asked **D**. "Why not?"

"Because Be is always right.
But, I will prevail," cried Hate.
"I swear that I'll taste my delight
in the darkness some night."

Well, unconsciously **D** so missed his delight,
he cursed with all of his might,
"I hate Be, too."

"That's good," praised Hate, beckoning to Evil waiting nearby.
"Hey, **D**, this is my friend, Evil."

"Should I call you Master Evil?"

"Oh, no," deferred Evil. "Hate is the 'Master of Disaster.'
I am Evil, but my friends just call me 'Bad E,' so call me Bad E, **D**."

Relieved that he had made another friend,
D replied, "I'll stick by your side from beginning to end."

"Can't wait," said Evil, winking at Hate.

Chapter 8

CONFUSION

The Counterfeits

Well, **D** earnestly employed Hate's Undo Curse.
Consequently, his attitude grew steadily worse.

So, feeling out of sorts and longing to belong,
D asked Hate to sing him a song.

"What?" replied Hate. "Are you kidding?
We don't sing in Un!"

"Why not?"

"There's no harmony here; we can't carry a tune.
But I'll tell you what: my stinger can croon," Hate declared sarcastically.

What's your stinger?"

"It's my beastly sting that causes real pain."

With irresistible curiosity, **D** asked, "How about the stinger and you just croon a refrain? Really, any ol' ditty would do."

"Alright, **D**, this one's for you."

Then Hate and his stinger crooned:

> "We're so bad we're despicable;
> we're destructive, unpredictable;
> We're cruel, harsh, deceitful, and vicious.
> To sum it up: we're deliciously malicious!"

"Oh, sting it again," sadly whimpered the lonely **D**. "Please, let's sting it again and again."

So they did.

Consequently, with each and every hateful word,
D's vision grew more distorted and blurred.

Sometime later, **D** complained to Bad E, "I can't see straight."

"It's all Be's fault," responded Evil.
"Why don't you retaliate — take control of fate and redesign Be's Alpha-beat scene?"

"Be's Alpha-beat scene? I don't know what you mean. Can I see it?"

"No — it's invisible to us here in Un."

"Why?"

"Because it's a realm of ideas."

"What's an idea?"

"An image in thought."

"Whose thought?"

"Be's thought," said Evil. Then, goading **D**, Evil added,
"But those poor ideas, limited by good, should have a choice."

"You mean they don't have a voice?" asked **D**.

"No voice, no choice, and no physique to speak of, either," confirmed Evil.
"They can't even choose between good and bad!"

"You sound mad," said **D**.

"Just sad.
But if you redesign that exclusive Alpha-beat line,
it will restore your distorted sight and dim Be's annoying bright light!"

"Alright," vowed **D**. "I will do something about the Alpha-beat's lack of choice!"

So, **D** began gathering data
on Be's exclusive neighborhood,
perusing it obsessively,
while up to no good.

"This Alpha-beat is my enemy," fumed **D**.

"Besides, nobody there looks a bit like me.
They're just ideas, all physique-free,
while I'm stuck with these debilitating knees.
They should have to serve Un, just like me!"

Zealous with jealousy, he vowed, "I'll get even with Be.
I will outline each Alpha-beat letter and confine it with a 'him' or 'her' fetter!"

D ruminated, fussed, and fumed feverishly.
Eventually, rage consumed his demented thought.
It was black and thick and fraught with rot.

Inflamed, the rage fabricated smoke that began to choke **D**.

But, delirious, he refused to stop
until the smoke vented straight up, right out of his top.

Then slowly, masterfully, using the smoke to malign,
D outlined each idea-letter that Be had designed.

To each formerly physique-free letter he assigned a "new norm,"
with a personality enclosed in a physical form.

They were capital letters with quizzical shapes:
some were quite straight,
and five had a top;
seven had curves,
and one didn't stop.
Half were female, and the rest were male.

With pride, **D** cried, "I will prevail!"

That said, **D** felt powerful, and it went to his head!

Focusing intently on each letter — including one for Be — eventually brought
that letter to life in **D**'s imagination.

With Time's assistance, he came to see their identities correspond to his
skewed point of view.

"Done," proclaimed **D**.

And then, with his twisted mind, **D** maligned his own design, decreeing,
"If a letter won't conform to me, I'll deform it."

Finally, **D** named his contorted collection of physical male and female letters
the "Beta-beat" show;
here's the whole fraudulent formation lined up in a row:

ABC EFGHIJKLMNOPQRSTUVWXYZ

And so, in the imaginary life of Un,
the counterfeit of Be's Alpha-beat Language of Life had begun.

"Good work, **D**; now darkness will live in infamy," congratulated Evil with a grin.
"And soon, the real fun will surely begin."

"Thanks, Bad E. Now I know the formula for disaster and destruction,"fumed **D**,
as he choked on his self-induced smoke.

As the smoke of corruption began to expel, Evil took off, coughing,
"Jeez, **D**, this is swell! Wait here while I get the cartel."

Chapter 9

Reverie

In a flash, Time, Evil, Hate, and Fear appeared.

"We've come to inspect your Beta-beat," Hate announced,
and then proceeded to march up and down the row,
scrutinizing each letter from head to toe.
"This is quite a feat," he repeated quietly to Evil, "quite a feat, indeed."

"It looks complete," offered Time.

"Are these 'Beats' elite?" asked Hate.

"I believe they're first rate," declared **D**.

"In that case, you'd better attach disabling labels of lack," instructed Evil, maligning **D**'s feat.

"What's a 'label of lack'?"

"A negative word that destabilizes and disables."

"How do I attach a disabling label?" asked **D**.

"Come here," ordered Hate, slapping **D**'s back and droning in his ear,
"For labels to stick, you have to fill 'em with fear."

"You mean smear 'em," responded **D**, peering at Fear, who was cowering in the corner.
"Why fear?"

"Fear defrauds, falsifies, and feigns pain," explained Hate. "It's our offensive strategy."

Feeling tense and tired, **D** then inquired, "Well then, fear of what?"

"Words!" instructed Fear.

"Words like: chronic . . . acute . . . death . . . pollute . . . and . . . institute," continued Evil
with its reverberating voice. "At last there's a reason down here to rejoice."

"Wait — why institute?" asked **D**.

"Allowing their original purpose to rest on the shelves,
institutes gradually live to serve mostly themselves," explained Evil with glee.
"Then we begin to move in and, with the aid of bureaucracy, eventually win."

At that point, a fog-like smoke ushered in its confusing reign,
as **D** was declared a "hero" in Un's undulating domain.

"You're a hero!" cheered the cartel.

"What's that?" asked **D**.

"The focus of praise," answered Evil.

"Thanks, but I really have nothing to say," said **D**, departing defeated and frayed.

"He's lost his delight," they snickered, watching their "hero" flicker out of sight.

Thus, dazed by the haze of the cartel's mesmerizing reign,
D became the "But" of Un's malevolent disdain.

"We must remember this date," ticked Time to Evil, Fear, and Hate.

"And just wait," predicted Fear. "The absence of good is about to appear!"

Chapter 10

COLLUSION

Heartless

Exhausted, **D** fell into a deep sleep, dreaming about the Beta-beat and Be.

"Even though I have commandeered and depleted Be's Alpha-beat,
my Beta-beat design still isn't mine.
I must own them, heart and soul; I must have the sole control.

"There just isn't room for two creators; only one will do.
I alone must exude the Mastermind glow; therefore, Be has simply got to go.

"I must blot out every thought of Be.
First, Be must be erased, then replaced with the Beta-beat **B**,
and then everything, including **B**, will eventually be governed by me.

"Because this is my dream, and I am supreme and can do what I want.
Therefore, as of this moment, on this auspicious occasion,
I officially erase Be and the invisible Alpha-beat from the entire equation.

"And in their place, the Beta-beat and **B** will be all that we see.
The original Be will dwell forgotten — put way out of sight,
making way for darkness to dictate the counterfeit right.

"I will overtake the Beta-beat line and undermine their self-worth and identity."

Thus, having gained serenity, and with the help of Time,
D imagined himself in command of **B**'s Beta-beat line.

"Wow!" he drooled. "All of this will be mine."

Surveying **B**'s beautiful domain, **D** felt the perturbing pain of exclusion,
and this gut-wrenching sting instigated his worst conclusion — yet.

"I must upset **B**'s set-up!" he vowed.
"But how?"

Just then, observing **B** singing with **E**, **D** sarcastically scoffed, "Humph, **BE**."

And later, overhearing **W** whistling with **E**, **D** plotted,
"To get what I lack, I'll devise a fable and pass it as fact."

He reasoned that if the Beta-beat would oppose good, he could depose **B**.

"I must deflect **B**'s benevolent beam now . . . but how?"

Then, in the darkest hour of night, **D** dug down deep and got it just right.

"I know," he thought.

"I'll fabricate a *façade* called fraud,
which covers up good with a falsifying fog of insinuations and lies."

And that comprised his plan.

ILLUSION

Guilt

With his dream-plan in hand to subvert the Beta-beat,
D got right down to the business of defeat.

Cozying up to the curvaceous **C**, he whispered,
"Curses on your clarity and compassion!"

But no sooner had this curse left his lips,
than **D** found himself locked into one of guilt's vise-like grips.

"How can I assault **C**, a letter so cute and mellow?
I'll just have to pick on another Beta-beat fellow," he reasoned.

Then, comparing himself with **E**'s equilibrium and ease, **D** cried in pain,
"Enough! I don't have enough!" And this thought really hurt him as he concluded,
"I must not be good enough."

Infuriated, he fumed, "Well, I may not be equal to **E**, but I swear I'll get even.
I will impair **E**'s ability to think,
bringing the whole of **BE** and **WE** to the brink — of despair!"

This devilish thought so tickled his fickle fancy
that **D** laughed right out loud,
with a sinister sound
that rebounded
and echoed within the borders of Un.

And that uproarious laugh woke him up from his dream!

"Wow! That dream seemed real, and now I feel ready to evolve,"
thought **D**, steadying his resolve.

"But how do I get the power to impair?" he wondered. "With mist?"

"Pssst!" whispered Evil, haunting his thought. "This is what you want."

"What is it?"

"My hypnotic, super-duper mental serum."

"What's that?"

"Our uppity key to superiority over **B**."

"How does it work?" asked **D**.

"Any self-righteous, arrogant, unfounded Beta-beat opinion
tips the balance and gives us dominion."

"How?"

"When wrong, their power belongs to us; when right, they have all the might."

"You mean, our might is a sham —our 'power' only resistance, a dam?"

Irritated by the question and tone of **D**'s voice, Evil groaned impatiently,
"The Beats disown their might when they mistake wrong for right."

"Consequently, their every wrong makes us strong?"

"That's Un's theme song," confirmed Evil.

"So, with one inflicting prick,
this hypnotic serum makes them believe they're superior or sick."

"That's the trick," confirmed Evil, "and where your power to hypnotize lies.
Now get along with your deed."

"Thanks for the serum," said **D**. "It's just what I need."

And Evil agreed. "Our favorite fault results in just one word: 'guilty.'"

"So it's all about 'guilt.'
I have felt guilty, and now I see how to use it. Thanks, Bad E."

All charged up, **D**'s response was to giggle with malevolent glee!

Having finally reached his zenith of zeal, **D** squealed, "Tonight, I will find my delight
by infecting **E**'s complexion with unequaled self-centered affection.

"I'll just expand my imaginative power
and hypnotize them all within the very next hour."

39

As this tale unfolds, a question may arise about the whereabouts of Be.

Be assured, dear reader, that Be as Being is always present.

However, it is not Be's way to interfere with this imaginary tale,
for in it each letter chooses to flourish, flounder, or fail.

Their decisions determine the way each will go —
either to remain in the light or depart into woe.

So don't blame Be if the letters go astray.
They each own their conclusions at the end of the day.

Chapter 12

INTRUSION

The Undoing

As the Beta-beat slept on their bedrock of Being, they dreamed.

Fantasizing himself into **E**'s dream,
D observed her singing a duet with **B**.

As **E** sang innocently, **D** injected Evil's
hypnotic serum of superiority into her unsuspecting thought,
and, unprotected, she accepted it as her own!

"Yes, I do have an unusually beautiful voice," professed **E**.
"Compared to the rest, I believe **B** likes mine best.
Although all our voices are divine,
no other is equal to mine."

"Guilty of duplicity!" judged **D**, observing the imbalance and vanity of her dream.
"Now I can curse with malaise,
while dissing her with my malevolent gaze."

Then, staring at her hypnotically,
D decreed, "Curses upon you, **E**. You're evil."

And before anyone could tell, **E** fell under the spell of the Death-Wish Cartel.

Finding it impossible to think,
she was still, however, able to smell **D**'s narcissistic stink.

40

"Eek!" shrieked the hypnotized **E**, caught off guard.
"What's evil?
That's not a **B**-attitude of gratitude and peace."

"**B**-attitudes are *passé*," declared **D**.

"No way!" responded **E**, beginning to panic.
"I'd better ask **A**."

"**A** agrees with me," lied **D**.
"Evil is as real as good."

"Are you saying **A** thinks evil is equal with good?"

"Yes," affirmed **D**.

"Egad!" emoted **E**.
"Now I'm uneasy, and that's making me queasy."

"Good," replied **D**, as he began to depress and distress **E**.

"Please, don't dis my ease," pleaded **E**.

"Dis, dis, dis," hissed **D**, as **E** turned and fled.

But **D** sped after her with malicious intent,
and eventually she became demoralized as **D** deflated **E**'s demeanor —
without easing up.

"What's the use?" **E** later grieved to **C**.
"Evil has caused my ease to evaporate."

"I'm so sorry for your misfortune," sobbed **C** with compassion.
"You have my sincere sympathy."

As Evil's maleficent mist reappeared,
twisting
B's all-consistent state of truth,
D praised his own use of malaise.

So, with **E**'s and **C**'s acceptance of the hypnotic curse,
D began his Beta-beat reverse.

Chapter 13

The Trial

Following his successful infiltration, **D** deliberately set out to destroy
his own Beta-beat, by introducing **D**-conceptions such as:

depreciate, demoralize, and debilitate.

These new "double-talk" words — essentially, opposites to good —
produced darkened clouds of condescension,
which began to obscure the once ever-present clarity of
B's harmonious dimension.

O and **K**, unsettled by the discord, were the first to notice
the subtle decline in their universal feel-good freedom.
They had always expected it to be maintained,
for there had never been a single reason to complain.

Detecting departure from **B**'s precepts, **O** protested,
"These **D**-conceptions are not **B**-attitudes.
They're merely opposites, divisive or crude!
Harmony and goodness are what we exude.

"Mind you," **O** continued, "remain resigned to the letter of **B**'s original design."

In kind, **K** warned, "Don't fall for this foolery!
Don't you see, this **D** is trying to desecrate **B**."

"Take it easy," retorted **E** to **O** and **K**. "This is only harmless fun.
There is no end to what **B** has begun."

Consequently, deviant **D** continued to besmirch and berate the **B**-attitudes obsessively.
Fascinated by his derisive personality,
the other letters followed **D** — mostly out of curiosity.

"**D**'s double-talk denigrations and defamations are funny," said **F**. "They tickle my fancy."

"I think they're silly and cool," laughed **S**.
"Let's have some fun with the exception to the rule."

"Excuse me, **S**," exclaimed **X**.
"Any exception to the rule will make you a fool."

"What's wrong with just a little ridicule?" snapped **S** in response.

"Your excuses will result in abuses," warned **X**, exiting the crowd.

But mostly, the others agreed with **F** and **S** — at least openly —
for fear of not fitting in with "**D**'s Defects."

D was in style, while the **B**-attitudes were "rejects."

"Watch out!" cautioned **O** and **K** to the Beta-beats. "Beware!"

But they obviously didn't care.

"**B**, do something," urged **O** and **K**. "You're losing control."

"Don't you see," answered **B** privately,
"this outline called **B** is a counterfeit of the incorporeal Being that's free.
This is the form that **D** has conceived —
a misconception, an illusion, not a fact; don't agree.

"Being isn't defined by mist or dust,
so relax, watch, and learn how to trust.
Good is the law, and good will prevail.
Any attempt to undermine it is destined to fail.

"The letters will learn at the end of the day
that **D**'s ways are deadly and fraught with dismay.
When on 'empty,' they'll yearn to return;
and then they will say
that glitz and emotions and wayward devotions
are ill-conceived notions that rob and don't pay.

"Just remember, dear **O** and **K**, you always have an *out,*
because error has no essence, substance, or clout."

"We will follow your lead," stated **O**.

Nodding, **K** agreed.

As one can imagine with Time, what had been united and whole
became divided and depleted.

Even **X**, who had been excluded by the others,
defaulted to the peer pressure to exalt **D**.

The **B**-attitudes fell out of favor; **B**'s approval rating tanked, too.

Deviancy and defiance, coined the "new true,"
had become *de rigueur*
for fashion, etiquette, and custom.

"We've got to bust 'em," urged Time.

"Who?" asked Fear.

"**O** and **K**. Those nerds won't say derogatory words," complained Time.

Accordingly, based on the defiance of **O** and **K**,
and concerned that things just might not go their way,
the Death-Wish Cartel, malicious and vile,
suggested to **D** that he put "goodness" on trial.

"Let's defeat 'good' in the Court of Public Opinion.
This will restore our control and give you dominion," said Evil to **D**.

"Since this is Un, where I control the state,
I'll be the judge," volunteered the enthusiastic Hate.

"Use the Beta-beat to act as the jury,
and get them whipped up into a furious flurry!" suggested Fear.

"Now, get going," urged Time. "You know I don't like to be wasted!"

"But wait!" hesitated **D**. "Who is the defendant and the plaintiff?"

"As the plaintiff, **D**, you will attack 'good,'" instructed Hate.

"Who is the defendant?" asked **D**.

"Who's afraid to defend 'good'?" asked Evil, with anticipation.

"Well," thought **D**, "**B** hasn't defended her **B**-attitudes. I think she's afraid."

"Good!" cried Evil. "**B** will stand trial for not being good enough.
She will be the accused."

Soon, the court showdown began,
and both the Cartel and **D**
were almost delirious with glee.

"This Court of Public Opinion will come to order," commanded Hate.
"**B**, take the stand.
D, begin your questioning."

"Your friends, **B**, have renounced goodness," began **D** authoritatively.
"Why didn't you force them to stop?"

B quietly rose from her chair as the court became hushed with anticipation.

Standing ever upright, the silent **B** clearly was holding to
the Law of Perfection
that acknowledges Love as sustaining and maintaining the innocent.

"Speak," demanded **D**, again challenging **B** to condemn her friends.

All eyes and ears were on **B**, awaiting her response.

But, refusing to debate
the hallucinated state
of unreality and hate,
B said
nothing.

Understanding the foolishness of debating
nothing,
O and **K** followed suit.

The silence was deafening!

Finally, **D** broke the mesmerism by shouting to the jury,
"Quick! I'm in a hurry.
Pick your verdict!
Innocent or guilty?"

Fearful for the first time, the jurors said nothing.

"Your silence has spoken!
Guilty as charged," yelled Hate from the bench.

"You, **D**, have belittled, beaten, and defeated 'good'!"

"What have we done?" whispered **W** to **E**.

"Nothing," she replied.

"Case closed," pronounced Hate, pounding his gavel with a resounding whack.

"Our attack on 'good' is complete," declared Time.

"Soon 'lack' will be the 'new sublime,'" chimed in Hate.

From that fateful moment in Time, **D**,
dug in deep at the base he called Deadquarters,
threatened to deform and debase any letter that refused to
deify **D** and his Unreality.

It appears the Cartel's *Undo Coup D'etat*
had dethroned Be's Law …
of Good!

PHASE II

Chapter 14

The Deletion

Time passed,
and it soon became apparent that
the success of the coup was not entirely true.

A few of the Beta-beats refused
to bow and kowtow to **D**'s demands,
resulting in offhanded reprimands by the Cartel.

"Jeez, **D**," taunted Evil, "your command is abysmal."

"What's that mean?" asked **D**.

"Appalling! You'd better enthrall them," called Hate, while spying on the "Beats" from afar.

"What's 'enthrall' mean?"

"Enslave."

"Enslave 'em? Ooooh! Enslave!
Hate, you just gave me a clue," raved **D** with delight.
"Now I know exactly what to do, and will get to it."

Later that day, as an unidentifiable mass of depression
settled on Deadquarters in the darkening twilight of Un,
the determined **D** emerged from mission control to issue his first official decree.

"All Beta-beats must report quickly to Deadquarters," proclaimed the voice of **D** over the airwaves.

"This sounds grave," whispered **O** to **K**,
as they all quietly made their way to Deadquarters.

"What should we do?" asked **K**.

"I'll lead the way," whispered **O**.
"Follow me, not **D**."

With all the capital letters assembled in place,
D glared at each and every Beta-beat face.

Intending his decree to deem
the physical realm supreme over the mental,
D began to unroll his scroll of demands.

With dynamic flair he declared,
"i, **D**, am banishing all beta-beat ideas and Devising my own."

That evoked a rebellious groan from **O**.
But the rest just fearfully went with the flow.

Overlooking **O**'s outburst, **D**, taking a deep breath and clearing his throat,
recited by rote his first decree:

the Declaration of separation

whereas, you are now subject to my visible Design,

and whereas, you are no longer free from physical fetters,

you, henceforth, will be called the lowercase beta-Detter-letters.

therefore, be it known that all capital letters will Desist and Decease,

with the exception of me
(or by my personal Decree).

your Dictator,

D

"What?" gasped **W**.

Looking askance at **W**, who was still in capital form, **D** shouted,
"i repeat, all capital letters will Desist and Decease with the exception of *D*!"

"are you saying that it's illegal to:
1) capitalize the first letter of each sentence
2) capitalize our individual I
3) capitalize our names — now and forever?" queried **W** with disbelief.

"that's correct," thundered **D**. "if you must, take notes.
D is the only letter that shall be capitalized between quotes."

"the Deed is Done," declared **D**. "now i control un!"

And with that sentence,
the Beta-beat was instantaneously de-capitalized
in a darkened dust-cloud of strife
and unrivaled chaos.

When the dusty debris settled,
the "Detters"
beheld their lowercase letters:

abc efghijklmnopqrstuvwxyz

— maimed and shamed by **D**'s rancor and rage.

"you're all guilty of Duplicity," pronounced **D**,
"and condemned forever to irreversible, lowercase captivity."

"my will is ill," whimpered **w**, envisioning a future in violation
of the prescribed rules of standard capitalization.

"be still!" screamed **D**. "no Debate."

So they waited . . . and waited . . . with grave expectation.

"however," **D** finally stated, "so you don't feel Deprived, i do have a captivatingly new
concept for you."

At that moment, you could have heard an i . . . dot.

Continuing, **D** announced, "the concept is called . . .

choice.

"instead of boring be-attitudes,
you are now free to choose from my tempting menu of goods."

"what are your goods?" asked **x**.

"my goods are Delicious eye-candy, intoxicating, glitzy, and guaranteed to set you apart."

Defiantly, the rebellious **o** shouted, "No!"

"you Delinquent!" yelled **D**. "i ordered you to capitalize *D* words only!
no capital **n**'s are allowed!"

"Be good!" **o** bellowed in defiance.

"i'm afraid," wailed **c**.

"Don't be deceived, **c**," shouted **o**, with rising defiance.
"This coup will fail. Capital precepts always prevail!"

Then, turning to **c** and the other Beta-beats, **o** shouted,
"Repeat after me, 'No! No! No!'"

"omit him!" commanded **D**. "this rebellion must stop."

"No! No!" challenged **o**, *then deleted on the spot.*

The Beta-beat gasped, and their hearts . . . skipped a beat,
having just witnessed **o**'s shocking delete.

"why did **D** delete **o**, and where will he go?" whispered **j** to **k**.

But she just snapped, "out of my way, **D**," in response to his deed.

"i Don't need you, **k**; you're Dispensable," retorted **D**, undisturbed by her outburst.

"this is the worst of Days," whispered **p** to **q**.

"quiet," urged **q**. "who knows what he'll Do."

After that, they had nothing to say,
especially **k**, who simply catapulted away.

Now, reader, you may be wondering just where **o** and **k** went.

Don't lament! Every idea lives forever within Be's bright —
even if it seems to be way out of your sight.

50

Chapter 15

SUBSTITUTION

Day of Descent

With **o** and **k** now out of the way,
the Beta-beat core was down to twenty-four.

"without **o** and **k**, what will we do?" worried **u**.

D knew that for spelling to succeed,
o and **k**'s presence were definitely a need.

So he commanded, "Replacements!"
And, as if on cue,
a substitute **k** and **o** rolled right into view.

Balancing precariously atop the oscillating **o**,
this **k** had been dismayed from the very get-go.

"beta-Detter-letters, meet subs **k** and **o**," declared **D** with pride.

The Detters, grieving the loss of the original **o** and **k**, all tried not to cry.
But their tears soon welled up and over, running down each face
as, terrified, they knelt, trembling, in place.

Disgraced, **D** cried, "**k** and **o** are here to block
and knock out any memory of the former **o** and **k**.
remember, i am **D** and will have it my way!"

Taken aback at the sight of the Beats' weeping red eyes,
D's substitute **k** stared at them with suspicious surprise.

Then, as if to break the spell, she yelled,
"i Don't like this view or know what to Do!"

Trying to soothe **k**, **j** jabbed her with his jot.
"you're safe beside me; Don't move from this spot."

"but you've got a jot for a head," wailed **k**, cowering with dread.

"then look at my hook instead," suggested **j**, trying to allay **k**'s fear with joviality.

"**j**, jump to the rear," ordered **D**, annoyed by **j**'s steadfast sense of joy.
"you're just a backwards jerk with a personality quirk."

"i am?" reacted **j** with dismay.

> Admitting that lie into the core of his soul,
> **j**, so ashamed, wanted to dive into a hole.
>
> However, to the Beta-detters' surprise, subs **o** and **k**
> were not going to let **D** have it his way.

Suddenly **k** shrieked, "i Don't like your ways,"
as she fixated her anger on **D** with a glazed, gray gaze.

"**k**, beware of that haze," cautioned **u**,
sensing that the link to sub-**k**'s sanity was cracking in two.

> (Sadly, **u**'s premonition was about to come true.)

Now, angry to the brink of insanity, the sub-**k** of **D**'s fabrication screamed,
"you . . . you, **D**, . . . you're killing . . ."

> Then, to the horror of the Beta-detter crew,
> sub-**k**'s sanity snapped completely in two,
> filling the air with dread —
> and dead silence.
>
> With her deranged gaze,
> — now frozen in place in both time and space —
> sub-**k** stood transfixed and mixed,
> betwixt life and death.
>
> Holding their breath, the Detters stared at **k** in disbelief.
> With her face appearing off-kilter and dazed,
> she resembled a stone-cold statue,
> demented and crazed.

Apparently, sub-**k**'s fate had been preordained
by **D**'s unexplained malignant distain.

To further malign, **D** shouted, "i told you, **j**, get to the end of the line."

"i tried to warn **k** about the gray," whispered **j**,
comforting the distraught sub-**o**
as he jumped past him to the end of the row.

"what's the gray?" whispered **o** fearfully.

"the gray mist depresses until its victim obsesses."

"shut up, **j**," ordered **D**.

"oh no," moaned sub-**o**, rolling over and over to cope with his pain.

Dismissing the drama, **D** resumed, with feigned hospitality declaring,
"beta-Detter friends, you should refrain now from 'good,' and come sample the array of my
succulent goods."

"please repeat that," requested **c**, confused by **D**'s use and abuse of compassion.

"listen to me," shrieked **D** at the unsuspecting **c**.
"i have already told you once.
what are you, a crude, feckless Dunce?"

"me oh my," murmured **m**, as **D**'s rebuke was met with shivering silence.

That is, until **t** blurted, "please don't belittle my tittle," which was drooping with fright.

"you're a tedious teeny-weeny, **t**," screamed **D**, as **t**'s little tittle tapped to attention.

Witnessing these encounters paralyzed the Detters with panic.

"say something!" demanded **D**.

But they said nothing.

So, with hypnotic flair, **D** transformed himself into a lowercase **d**,
and with little **a** in tow, grabbed the decapitalized **b**
to form a previously inconceivable concept:

bad.

Now, **b**, with only **a** in between, was face to face with **d**!

And utterly deceived, the Detters saw what they believed.

To make matters far worse,
d deliberately enthroned the perverse by declaring:

"now that i have your attention,
it Delights me to mention
that what has been known as the lower-case **b** is, henceforth, banned altogether
and, consequently, will no longer exist as a beta-Detter letter."

"but . . . but . . . how will we spell words correctly without **b**?" asked **c** courageously.

"it's simple," responded **d**, glaring triumphantly at **b**.
"as you can plainly see, your Down-trodden **b**
is the mirrored image of me, your humble servant, **d**.
henceforth, the reverse image of *d* will substitute for every *b* word."

"that's absurd," thought **g**.

"so Do you get my gist?" concluded **d**.
"**b**, the beta-Detter-letter, will no longer exist."

And with this unbelievable twist of fate,
d began to erase **b** from the state
of their collective imagination.

But **b** took it in stride, knowing inside that all Being is permanent and perfect.

"now what will we Do?" murmured **u** as **b** was being obliterated from view.

Savoring his delusive victory, **d** proclaimed,
"now my universe is perverse, because there's good <u>and</u> bad!
and look, **t**: i'm a peewee **d**."

"is the 'bad' persona a mask?" wondered **w**, too terrified to ask,
as they knelt silently at attention that entire night of Descension.

Chapter Sixteen

DELUSION

Debauchery

As the depth of darkness negated any sense of dawn,
D recapitalized to his original size,
further traumatizing
them all.

"i feel small," sighed **t**,
who was used to standing tall.

This deliberate debauchery engendered the Beta-beat devolution,
magnetized by the gravity of
depravity, demoralization, and doubt.

"what a malevolent Deficiency," mocked **D**.
"**b** and the beta-beat have been separated and Defeated by me!"

~ ~ ~

Trying to cope
and hoping for the best,
the Beta-detters began to imbibe
D's dualistic discourse
of
good and bad.

Used to having a very good time,
y and **z** yipped and zipped
right off the deep end,
wanting to believe **D** wholeheartedly, and finding delight in being bad.

But soon, stronger potions of intoxication were demanded
to quench "bad's" insatiability.

Bad was causing pain.
Bad thinking was causing bad consequences,
and the Detters began to have bad thoughts
and to expect bad things to happen.

Disillusionment ensued, and the **y** and **z** duo despaired.

"i thought *bad* was supposed to feel good," yipped **y**.

"all this bad makes me sad," sighed the de-zipped, sedated **z**, dozing to dull the pain.

Duped by **D**, and judged "unacceptable" by **D**'s school of rules,
the expelled **y** and **z** opted to drop out.

"where will we go?" asked **y**.

"go to sleep," yawned **z**.

~ ~ ~

Believing **D**'s despotism would pattern the former **B**'s benevolence,
the Beta-detters developed all kinds of deficits.

Having thus naively discarded **B**'s bestowal of abundance,
they soon depleted each resource,
which forced them to lean on **D**.

As **D**'s addiction to dominance deepened,
he designated the Beta-detter-letters as the

"beta-Debt."

"now I *own* you because you *owe* me," declared **D**.

And from the very depth of their delusion, the enslaved beta-Debt cried,
"what happened?"

~ ~ ~

Soon, the Beta-debtors began to despair.
How had "bad" become the norm and "good" abnormal?

A few letters, still devoted to the b-attitudes, detected **D**'s derangement.
But, by this time, many of the letters had declined
to the point of resigned despondency.

The Debtors dreamed of Beta-better days, but feared the worst: *deletion*.

Deducing that their identities were being de-programmed,
they yearned to dissolve **D**'s lowercase detention.

"why can't we capitalize like **D**?" pouted **p**.

"that's a good question," agreed **t**.

"well maybe we'll be recapitalized," offered **i** with a sigh.

Immediately, an abrupt voice interrupted.
"capitalize, **i**, and all you Debtors will die."

Suddenly, a deafening command blared from Deadquarters.

"Debtors, line up and fall down."

Trembling, they scrambled to line up alphabetically,
then dropped to their knees.

Emerging from his lair
with a hypnotizing stare,
D intoned in his frigid, inflexible drone,
"the time has come to meet my invisible cartel mate.

"you shall call it 'Hate the great.' and take note:
the name *Hate* shall be capitalized;
all other **h** words shall remain undersized."

"is Hate a mistake?" murmured **m**.

"you can feel it," whispered **v** to **p**, "but you can't see it."

Thence, when Hate would blow in on the scene,
the Debtors perceived it as divisive and mean.

"i can't relate to Hate," whispered **w** to **x**.
"it confuses us and makes things complex."

"Hate separates," said **x**. "Don't trust it."

Hate's introduction promised more fear and dysfunction,
and **w** began wondering to herself:

"what can we trust?
where is what's just?

"who has the power to take or Destroy?
and why am i afraid to employ what was trustworthy before?

"when we adore what's passed from sight,
how Do we get it back from the night?

"and why am i afraid to speak up and take a stand?"

Unable to find answers or understand, **w** sighed,
"oh well, maybe later i'll Do what i can."

As Time wore on, one dismal night resolved into the next
until Hate,
and the fear of its dreaded sting,
weighed so heavily on the stilted letters
that they wilted.

But, welling up within with a desire to know,
w percolated the question the others were too fearful to mention.

"was there ever really a capital **b**?"

"no," insisted **D**.

"oh woe," winced **w**.

"capital **b** existed only in your imagination," scoffed **D**.

Having been put off, the hopeless letters
sank deeper and deeper into despair,
and, finally, just didn't even care
to think anymore.

And the Death-Wish Cartel, from its covered-up cell,
continued to conceal all that was real.

Chapter 17

DISILLUSIONED

Inspiration

Proud of their Devolution, the Death-Wish Cartel met at Deadquarters
to celebrate, evaluate, and review the results of the overall coup.

"that was easier than i thought," boasted Evil, who was bored to death by the stupefied
beta-Debtors dozing to ease the ache of their despondent existence.

"now what?" asked Time, hoping for a rest. "i'm beat!"

"we've just begun!
there's more to be done," snapped Evil.

"more?" said Fear with alarm.

"there must be foreign letters to corrupt with our fetters," declared Evil.
"be Didn't create just twenty-six letters.
when we find more unsuspecting alpha-beat states,
we'll infiltrate,
then infect, so our power will expand,
then command everything."

"what about be's 'language of life'?" asked Fear.

"the infectious lie we injected has been accepted.
soon, by and by be's language of life will indubitably Die," predicted Evil.

"what about **D**?" asked Hate.

"**D** is out-Dated. his Deed is Done.
the beta-Debt's Deflated and sleepwalking in un."

"what will happen to him?" asked Time.

"he'll Decay and fade away to nothing, and there he will stay.
come on now, what Do you say? let's begin right away."

So, off went the Death-Wish Cartel to quell any other Alpha-beats dwelling
within Be's realm,
leaving **D** to eventually fall asleep in his Deadquartered deep.

But the question remains, where is Be?

Well, as you might have guessed, Be is present, alert, ready, nearby
for all who seem assailed and derailed by the lie.

For Being is fundamental — the first cause, premise, and key.
Its only requirement is agreement with Be.

As Principle itself, Being is steadfast, intact, both the *be* and the *do,*
responding to all who demand the true view.

So have no fear, reader. The Language of Life is destined to speak.
It will uplift the downcast and strengthen the weak.

~ ~ ~

Meanwhile, Time's minutes kept ticking relentlessly toward its own dead end.
The hours in Un accumulated into days, then decades,
then into the interminable "when?"

Un's Time-bound climate, so heavy-hearted and dark,
displayed nary a hint of one dissenting spark.
As the beta-Debt dozed more and more to escape all their pain,
there was no need for **D** to assert his negative reign.

So, he dozed off and on, too.

As for **y** and **z**, they were still asleep.
Having followed **z**'s suggestion a long while back,
y and **z** had climbed into the sack, hoping to escape from **D**'s *bad* attack.

Yet, as **y** slept, night after night and year after year,
she dreamed of something better.

In her dreams, she discerned a Be-like brightness
dispelling the mist with persistent uprightness.

This discernment beckoned her to awake.

"i want to wake up," yawned **y**, stretching her arms way out wide.
i'm tired of this nightmare
and want to begin anew.
but who am i, and why,
and what can *i* Do?"

And then this inspiration dawned upon her receptive thought:
"there must have been a beginning . . .
so there must have been a **b** . . .
so **b** from the beginning might still be here with me."

Then, with yearning **y** yelped,
"help, **b**, wherever you are."

And with an ensuing plea, she asked,
"why was i conceived, **b**?"

Wisely, **y** bided a reply.

Undaunted by a lack of response, she continued as her cry then amplified,
"why, **b**? why, why, why, why, *why*?"

With that call came the thought, "could lowercase **b** be a false view of capital **B**?"

With momentum, **y**'s cry magnified from "**b**?" to "**B**!"

And with that cry came the inspiration to ask, "Do i have the wrong conception of being?"

Imploring once more with great resolve, **y** called, "Be!"

With each sincere desire to know the true Be,
y's insight was refocused to see what Be sees.

By and by, this desire was blessed
with the certainty of Be's ever-present caress.

And as **y**'s understanding flowered,
it empowered fortitude to flow within from an indwelling fountain.

Swelling with the conviction of Be as the exclusive originator of all,
y called from the very bosom of her being,
"why was i created, Be? why, why, why, — *why*?"

Exhausted, she surrendered —
yielding her all to Be.

Then, with her thought securely ensconced, **y** got her response.

Welling from within **y** came Be's tender reply,
"Because, **Y**."

"you know my name?"

"You are my **Y**, **Y**, and nothing can change that fact."

As tears of gratitude flowed down her face,
y felt the smile of Be's loving embrace.

There in the dark
glowed the Primary Spark!

Then, ever so gently, Be's beam of truth
anointed the persistent **y** with the
balm of calm
that revealed these additional understandings:

y has never been lowercase.
y belongs only to Be.
y is not a question.
y is a fact of Being.

Suddenly, **y** deduced right out loud,
"there must be a reason for me to *be*,
and that reason is the truth about me. yippee!
but what is it, and what is my purpose in life?

"Be, i'm going to listen until i hear it,
and i promise i won't fear it.
i vow to pursue what you will have me Do."

y's heartfelt sincerity and devout concentration
were then rewarded with this revelation:

"My precious, youthful **Y**, you are a sleuth for truth."

"a sleuth for truth? why?" asked **y**.

"Because truth makes you free."

"how?"

"Through agreement with me."

"but how do i know what is true?" she wondered.
"could you please give me even one clue?"

"The right questions and answers will always make do."

"yes!" replied **y**. "questions and answers are what i'll pursue.
but what does being have to Do with cause?"

She continued to reason, "maybe it's cause and effect — the reason why things happen."

And after another long, thoughtful pause, she exclaimed,

"because!"

"that's it! i know the clue:
i'll investigate the word 'because' till i find out what's true!"

So, **y** devised a wise disguise to spy and sleuth for truth!

Chapter 18

CHOICE

o, i, c

Concurrently, at Deadquarters,
the lowercase thinking had degenerated so much
that even **D**'s delicious concept
choice
was losing its voice.

"choose, choose, choose," huffed **h**, numb and considerably dumbed down.
"how do you know what's good and what's bad?"

Neighboring **f** concurred, "yup, i'm mixed up, too.
what feels good isn't always good for you,
and realizing that you've been 'had' isn't always bad."

"what a mess," added **w**, walking by with **s**,
suggesting, "why not just guess?"

Fitting inside the beta-Debt row
was a problem for the "outsider," substitute **o**.
Having been commanded by **D** to be in the center of choice,
o had trouble finding his voice.

Noticing **o**'s discomfort, **c** asked, "what's bothering you, **o**?"

"kind of you to notice," said **o** shyly. "i . . . i feel like a misfit."

"what Do you mean?"

"my origin is Different; Don't think i fit in.
i'm boring, unusual, alone, with no kin."

"oh," replied **c**, "i Disagree. you're unique for a reason.
your individuality is original, intelligent — always in season."

"really?" asked **o** hopefully.

"of course," answered **c**. "and to show that i know,
you'll henceforth be known as our very own — not on loan — ,
well-toned and un-cloned, second-gen **o**."

"thanks," said **o**, "and if i'm officially the second-gen **o**, let's call the first one, 'original **o**.'"

"alright," confirmed **c**, "original **o** it will be! but Don't say that in front of **D**."

"why?"

"anything 'original' has been Declared illegal."

"thanks, i'll be careful," concluded **o**.

Now feeling officially accepted by the Debtors and appreciated for his service,
o was honored to stand in for the original **o**,
who had been deleted on Descension Day.

Like the original **o**, this replacement **o** possessed
an independent mind
designed
to think, and think, and think.

"stop thinking, **o**!" shouted **D**, passing by on surveillance. "it's illegal; you're unlicensed."

64

"yes sir, **D**, if you say so," replied **o** under duress.

But later that day, **o** opined to himself,
"it's oppressive here in **choice**, just going around in circles.
i know i can think of a better way to go."

And think he did,
until he realized that **D**'s oppression
was, in fact, an opportunity!

This inspiration led him to ask the following questions:

Q: "is good ever bad?"
A: "no!" reasoned **o**. "bad is never the way to go."

Q: "is choice an illusion?"
A: "yes! it's a mockery of choice because we have no voice."

Q: "have we fallen for this illusion?"
A: "yes!" was **o**'s conclusion. "we have fallen asleep."

Q: "are we Deluded?"
A: "yes, Deluded and, therefore, excluded from good."

Q: "what's the way out of Delusion?"
A: "we must become Disillusioned with the Delusion!"

Thus inspired, this second-gen **o** decided to act.

Empowered, **o** whispered to **i** at his side, "i'm going to Defect from **D**'s Disaster."

"really?" **i** replied. "i feel Disconnected. can i Defect with you?"

Overhearing **o** and **i**, **c** confessed, "look at me — incomplete."

c was seeking wholeness.

Gaping at the gap in her midriff, she declared,
"i want to find myself. can i Defect, too?"

"we're at the center of **choice**," pointed out **o**,
"and if we three Defect, it will be the end of it."

"that's right," agreed **i**.

"well, let's begin," said **c**, eager for a change of venue.

Just then, **o** got a big idea. "oh, oh, oh," he shouted, "original **o**!"

"shush" they whispered, knowing it was illegal to say "original" with anything but **D**.

And they shivered, knowing that if detected,
they'd be detained in **D**'s Deep Freeze of Fright indefinitely.

"how Did there get to be two **o**'s?" asked **i**.

"Don't know," answered **o**. "let's ask the original **o**."

"i thought the original **o** was Deleted," whispered **c**.

"he was, but i know he must still be around, because he chose good," restated **o**, inspired by intuition. "maybe he can help us."

"maybe he can reconnect us with **B**," whispered **c**.

"are you kidding?" objected **i**. "there is no **B** or **b**; she was erased by **D**."

"we'll see. come on, guys.
Departing from **D** sounds like a good choice to me," declared **o**.

But only **c** agreed.

"you go first; i'll wait till later," reneged **i**, deciding to play it safe.

Chafing at the bit, **c** whispered to **o**, "well, when will we go?"

"we'll know when the time is right," whispered **o**.
"but for now, let me wish you good night."

SERENDIPITY

Deep Freeze

Near Deadquarters, at the Border of Dim,
deep in the Land of Un,
D had developed with fiendish insight
a terrible thing called the Deep Freeze of Fright.

And often at night, **D** would pick out a Debtor
for a battle of wits to see who could spell better.
If his Debtor guest failed the test,
into the Freezer he'd go for a night of unrest.

This particular night, **D** picked **i** for the fight,
bellowing, "spell every word that includes an 'l.'"

Repelled, **i** just wanted to exit pell-mell.

"this Deep freeze is scary," quavered **i** with terror.
"i suppose i'll be frozen if i make even one error."

As **i** began spelling the words containing an "l,"
D anticipated **i**'s failure and thought it was swell.

"you aren't doing so well," taunted **D** with glee.

Proportionately as **i** became more fearful, his jot grew rigid and taut,
with each succeeding answer requiring more thought.

"there's no hurry," yawned **D**. "what could be nicer than spelling with me?
let's see — why, you're only at word number 183.
but it's late and i'm tired, so i'm going to bed.
spread out in the Deep freeze — here's a pencil and pad;
fill it up by the morn or you're gonna feel bad."

So **i** sat . . . and sat . . . and sat in the frozen deep,
all the while not sleeping a peep.

With the dawning of dusk, his jot was sore and inflamed,
and **i** indicted **D** as the one to be blamed.

That frigid night in **D**'s Deep Freeze did the trick,
and **i** was determined to defect, even though he felt sick.

While **i** was confined in **D**'s Freezer of Fright;
o and **c** listened all night for when to take flight.

"i think the time is right and that **i** may be ready to go,"
whispered the intuitive **o**.
"most likely he's still in the freezer of fright;
i bet he's been there for most of the night."

"alright, **o**," agreed **c** optimistically, "i'm ready to go."

In the dim light of morn as they drew near the Freezer,
they heard the unceasing wheezing of a volatile sneezer.

o cracked open the door, and there on the floor
was **i**, stiff, sore, and frozen to the core.

"tha, tha, thank goodness you're here," shivered **i**, recognizing **o** and **c**.

As **i**'s teeth chattered, his confidence shattered, he cried,
"plea, plea, please, get me out before **D** comes back, ack, ack,
or all three of us will be un, un, under attack.

"we must escape from this pla, pla, place without leaving a trace!
if you're ready to flee, i'll jo, jo, join and make three."

"good," cautioned **o**. "we'll wait, and go when i know it's time.
meanwhile, let's thaw you from this frostbitten crime."

"thank yo, yo, you, sub **o**. you know," smiled **i**, "you're all righ, righ, right."

And the genuine, heartfelt warmth of **i**'s compliment quite delighted **o**,
instantaneously thawed **i**,
and awed **c**.

"i just saw **i** thaw," exclaimed **c** incredulously. "how Did that happen?"

68

Somewhat refreshed, **o** and **c** helped **i** off the floor,
hoping they wouldn't see **D** anymore.

Then, moving cautiously out through the space,
they returned to **choice**, resuming their place.

~ ~ ~

Their chance to escape Dim arose that very night
while **D** jousted with **j** in their weekly Deep Freeze fight.

D commanded, "**j**, spell all the words that include an **a**,
or spend the next day . . . and night . . .
in my freezer of fright, along with **i**, who is still trying to get his assignment right."

"i'm feeling uptight," confessed **j**, overwhelmed by the task. "this jousting is confusing."

"are you losing your joy?" taunted **D**. "poor boy.
ya know i won't ever be fooled by that ploy."

"i suppose, by the end of the Day, you'll have it your way," sighed **j**.

"that's right," snickered **D**. "now Do what i say."

Thus began **D**'s degrading joust, designed to oust **j**'s remaining joy.

That task completed, **D** retreated to Deadquarters.

"with **j**'s joy dead, now i'm ready for bed," yawned **D**, falling into a deep sleep.

~ ~ ~

Meanwhile, having mustered what courage they could,
o, **i**, and **c** searched
and scouted for an exit out of Dim.

As they passed the intuitive **y**,
she inwardly cried,
"it's time to spy for truth!"

Wide awake, spry little **y** sleuthed undetected behind the unsuspecting trio.

"how do we get out of here?" asked **c**.

"steer clear of all fear," replied **o**.

"but you can feel the fear right here.
it's misty, and Dense, and it's making me tense," complained **i**.

Still stuffy and wheezy, **i** was feeling a bit sneezy
from his recent Freezer Fright scare.

So, while sniffing the night air,
he inhaled a whiff of despair,
which caused a deafening sneeze —
bringing him to his knees —,
and as the others stared,
his jot blew up in the air.

"ah . . . ah . . . ahhhhhhh-choooooo!"

"shhhhh!" whispered **o** on the spot,
as **i** jumped up to recover his jot.

As **i**'s blown-up jot settled back in its spot, **o** exclaimed,
"oh my! look what we've got."

The force of **i**'s sneeze had blown a hole in their illusion of harm,
a hole so big they could pass through arm in arm.

Fearing that **D** heard **i**'s sneeze back at the Deep Freeze,
and concerned that if caught they'd be erased,
the trio quickly jumped through the hole and kept going — posthaste.

"where are we going?" whispered **i**.

"to find the original **o**," answered **o**, rolling on ahead of **i** and **c**.
"i think he can help set us free."

"how can he free us?" asked **c**.

"original **o** is Double-o good," declared **o** emphatically, "like in the word 'good.'"

"and?" questioned **i**, waiting to hear **o**'s logic.

"and since goodness is a capital concept, original **o**, being a capital concept, must still be a capital letter, even though he was omitted as a lowercase Detter," concluded **o**, with insight and recall that surprised them all.

"wait — i Don't remember why he was omitted," confessed **i**.

So, to refresh their memory, **o** described the original **o**'s
omission on Descension Day, when he
was decapitalized and deleted.

"it was so terrible that i must have repressed it," confessed **i**.
"what happened?"

"**o** chose to stand up for good," explained the substitute **o**, adding,
"to stand for the good
of the whole neighborhood."

"you mean he didn't roll over?" asked **i**.

"nope," answered **o**.

"but didn't that happen before you arrived?" interrupted **i**.
"Did you contrive this?"

"no way! **k** and i were waiting in the wings of **D**'s imagination to replace any omission,"
explained **o**. "**D** had fabricated us for his substitute line,
in case **o** and **k** fussed, fought, or resigned."

"i remember **o** confronting **D**
and being Deleted while he stood up for me,"
wailed **c**, with compassion for **o**'s capital punishment.

"now i understand why **o** is 'the man;'
he took a real courageous stand for originality
by opposing **D**'s decree 'to be or *not* be.'"

"and there's more," **o** continued.
"i heard it told that the original **o** scolded **D**, saying,
'you can omit me, but you'll never Destroy good.'"

71

"i sure respect him for his loyalty to good," marveled **i**.

"original **o** might look lowercase now,
but it's been said that he's still endowed with s-o-u-l," spelled the prodigious **o**.

"s-o-u-l," spelled **c** very slowly. "soul . . . that word sounds vaguely familiar."

"i can kind of Define it, if you'd like," offered **o** shyly.

"oh yes, please try," replied **c** and **i**.

> "soul is the creative cause of all individual life,
> the animating principle precluding all strife.
>
> "soul is our nature, giving morals and motion
> that determine our selfhood, joy, and devotion.
>
> "soul is growth and perpetual progression,
> the essence that inspires our every expression.
>
> "soul illumines, enlightens, and loves everything.
> in short," concluded **o**, "soul composed the song we were created to sing!"

> And with their faint discernment of soul, the decapitalized trio received
> a glimmer of hope from the infinite scope
> of that long-forgotten concept.

Feeling soul singing throughout her whole body with holy bravura, **c**, a true coloratura, naturally burst into song:

> "i know something good is ahead,
> and there's no reason for fear or for dread;
> so for truth we shall progressively go,
> till we find our true friend, our original **o**!"

"what was that?" asked **o**, staring at the stunned little **c**, who didn't know she could sing.

"i Don't know," answered **i**, "but it sounded good."

"it just flowed right through me," explained **c**. "and it felt good, too."

"we must be on the right track," declared **o**. "stay focused."

"ok!" they exclaimed. "let's go find the original **o**!"

ENLIGHTENMENT

The Library

After what felt like forever, the trio,
with **y** gliding silently behind,
suddenly spied something magnificent.

Having kept her distance,
y, the spy, sensed something big
was about to blossom.

"look up ahead," shouted **i**. "there's a strange sight."

"could it be what was formerly called 'bright'?" asked **c**,
shielding her eyes from its radiant light.

"let's investigate," cheered **o**. "we Don't have too far to go."

As they approached the site,
they were led to a warehouse
emanating a glorious light.

"i think we need to look in here," whispered **o**, as the others nodded in agreement.

They cautiously made their way to the steps
of an immense, vaulted structure containing
volumes of letters, words, and books
with ideas so inherently true
that the whole warehouse naturally beamed
with an iridescent hue.

The trio, awed by the amazing vastness of this remarkable tomb,
stood dumbfounded in disbelief as they gazed in each room.

"Do you think this is where **D** hides the omitted, committed,
and independent concepts?" asked **c**.

"hey, look: what Does that sign say over the Door?" asked **o**.

"'library of the illegal,'" read **i** slowly, after his eyes had adjusted to the light.

"these ideas must be contrary to **D**'s Decrees," said **o**.
"there's probably more;
let's go in and explore."

Sneaking quietly in, they looked around carefully
until **i** spotted the *Dictionary of Deletes*.

"look, a book!" pointed **i**, who began pulling the dusty volume off the shelf so they could
have a closer look. "maybe original **o** is in here!" he exclaimed excitedly.

o rolled his eyes over the pages, and saw words like
honesty, ingenuity, morality, and the like.

Whistling in surprise, he exclaimed, "look at all these overlooked and undervalued
concepts!"

"why, these look like ignored and forgotten qualities of good," observed **i**.

They continued searching, until **c** recognized
original **o**'s rounded shoulders
in the "o" section of the *Dictionary*.

"hey! there's the original **o**!" whispered **c** with hushed excitement.

"where?" asked **o**.

Pointing at him with his jot, **i** said, "**o** is listed right there, after OJT!"

"what's OJT?" asked **c**.

"it says, 'on-the-job training,'" read **i**.

"what's on-the-job training?"

"it means learning while you work," said **o**.

"no wonder OJT is in here," said **i**. "we're not learning anything,
which explains why nothing works."

74

"noted," whispered **c**. "but look who's next to **o**! it's his Devoted sidekick, **k**!"

"hooray," whispered **i**. "they're listed together as '**ok**.'"

"but they're lowercase, like us," stewed **c**.

And indeed, that was true.

"at least we've found them," **i** sighed with relief. "i'm glad they survived!"

"should we speak to them now?" asked **c**.

"no, let's think on it for a while, and figure out how to greet them in style," suggested **o**, hoping to make a good first impression.

"wait! they're just listed in this book on a page. how do we know they're still alive after the omission?" asked **i**. "how are we supposed to talk to them?"

"let's walk through the *Dictionary* and find out. when we see OJT, then we'll know they're next," answered **o** with optimistic intellect, "and we'll see for ourselves if they survived."

So, finally beginning to thrive,
they hugged each other — happily revived.

Chapter 21

RESOLUTION

The Malignant Deception

Scrunching down real flat,
o, **i**, and **c** slipped onto the first page of the *Dictionary*.

As the trio embarked on their journey through the *Dictionary of Deletes*,
o and **k** were reminiscing about the glory days
when they had been Be-knighted as
Beacons of Light
and
Porters of Perfection.

Back then they had been entrusted to award the
Official **OK** Seal of Approval.

Together, they performed three specific duties:
1) Sticking to the letter of the original good design,
2) Encouraging infinitely creative and harmonious concepts, and
3) Detecting imitations.

When these duties were fulfilled, they delighted in awarding
the official **OK** Seal of Approval.

"I sense those good days will soon return," declared original **o** to **k**.

"I yearn to see the good return," agreed **k**. "And why not today?"

The trio, with **y** behind, maneuvered through
column after column,
row after row,
and page after page
of censored ideas and attitudes,
as they kept a lookout for the OJT that signaled **o** and **k**'s location.

Moving just past the center of the book, they heard **o** and **k**
singing the ballad that recalled the events on Descension Day.

"listen," said **o**. "there's that sound again."

"what is it?" said **i**.

"shhhh!" whispered **c**, turning in the direction of the singing. "let's listen."

The Ballad of **O** and **K**

k: "On Descension Day, as you rolled to jail,
I observed your face growing frightfully pale."

o: "You observed my face growing frightfully pale."

k: "Blimey, my mate's just rolling away,
but I'm sticking with **o**, no matter what **D** might say."

o: "You were sticking with me no matter what **D** might say."

k: "I cried, 'help me, Be; send me good, I pray.'
And sure enough, the good unrolled right away."

76

o: "And sure enough, the good unrolled right away."

k: "'Because you're free,' sang Be, 'break away from this plot,
because it's only a dream, and a captive you're not.'"

o: "'You're free,' sang Be. We broke away from the plot,
because it's only a dream and captives we're not."

o and **k**: "Doo, dah, doo, doodah, living like we should.
Doo, doo, doo, doodah, Be's only good. Yeah!"

Then, **o** rolled and **k** kicked up high,
much to the amazement of the trio and the spy.

"look, they're capitalizing the first letter of each sentence," cried **i**.
"they're rebelling against **D**'s rules!"

Surprised by their disregard for **D**'s law, **c** whispered,
"how can they be so happy when they've been Deleted?"

"it's the effect of having that s-o-u-l," spelled **o** as the duo resumed singing.

o: "Then Truth cut through fear's mental noose,
propelling Capital **k** to break away loose."

k: "The fear was gone and I broke away loose.

o and **k**: "So we're sidekicks here, each the other's recluse,
and though deleted and defrocked, we'll make no excuse,
because we know we'll get 'the call' and be put to good use."

o: "I'm free," sang **o**. "I broke away from the plot,
because it's only a dream and a captive I'm not."

k: "And I'm free," sang **k**. "We broke away from the plot,
because it's only a dream and captives we're not."

o and **k**: "Doo, doodah, doo, doodah, living as we should.
Doo, doo, doo, doodah, Be's only good! Yeah!"

"my oh my," thought **y**.
"**o** and **k** have maintained the commitment to soul
in spite of **D**'s Despotic control."

77

The duo's big hearts, though outwardly barred,
still beat with the glory days when capital **B** starred.

They were waiting patiently for each Beta-debtor-letter
to awake from its drama-like dream,
to reclaim its legal place on **B**'s capital team.

Just then, the trio spotted OJT,
with the gleaming "dream-team" duo
next in the row.

"hey-ho, original **o**!" called **o** excitedly. "can you lend us a hand?"

"Even though I look belittled, you can call me 'Big,'" responded **o** with a grin.
"Hey, **k**, take a look at who's rolling on in!"

Then Big **o** exclaimed, "What's your name?
And, by golly, our shape is the same!"

"well, if you're big **o**, then you'd better call me little **o**,"
replied Little **o** with humility and respect.

"And you can call me 'Coach **k**,' because I like it that way," grinned **k** happily.
"Now what can we do for you?"

"big **o** and coach **k**," whispered Little **o**, looking fearfully over his shoulder,
"we want to overthrow **D**."

"we want our independence," sighed **i** quietly.

"we want to be capitals again," added **c** emphatically.

"can you help us find capital **b**?" asked Little **o**.

Big **o** chuckled as **k** replied, "We didn't know she was lost!"

"But seriously," continued Big **o**, "why capital **B**?
Why not capital **E**, or **V**, or **Z**?" he asked, testing the trio's reasoning.

"because capital **b** represents everything that's good and right and true," said Little **o**,
"and we need to know her better so we can be more like **b**."

"maybe capital **b** can make us capitals again," added **c** with some uncertainty.

Pleased with the trio's resolve, Big **o** and Coach **k**
exchanged knowing glances, as if to say, "We're getting 'the call.'"

So they began telling **o**, **i**, and **c** stories
about the glory days of Capital **B**.

"but **b** was Decapitalized and erased," interrupted **c**. "we saw it happen!"

"You <u>think</u> you saw that because you were hypnotized by Time," explained Big **o**.

"what does it mean to be hypnotized?" asked **i**.

"To be seduced by a lie," replied Big **o**.

"And believe that it's true, and then let <u>it</u> do the thinking for you," added Coach **k**.

"you mean the lie masquerades as my thought?" asked the distraught **i**. "how does it work?"

"First, Time's hypnotic tick transfixes your imagination,
making you susceptible to any configuration," explained **o**.

"Second, Fear focuses your ears and eyes
on a duplicitous projection of lies and surprise," added **k**.

"Third, you believe that what you heard and saw was true,
which then determines all you think, say, and do," concluded Big **o**.
"It's as easy as 1, 2, 3."

"i see. well then, what <u>really</u> happened?" asked **c**.

"Capital **B** became invisible to you as you began to doubt her true identity.
You accepted the lie and believed it was true,
so the decapitalized **b** came into your view," said Big **o**.

"wait — if i'm a substitute **o**, Does capital **b** even know about me?" asked Little **o**.

"Oh yes, indeed. Capital **B** knows your original, capital identity as the real deal," said Big **o**.

"well then, how Do we get un-hypnotized? can we just change our mind?" queried **c**.

"Definitely," answered Coach **k**. "At any time, you can annul the dualistic curse by reversing
1, 2, 3 to 3, 2, 1, *and done*! I like to think of it as coming home to 'The One.'"

"But it's vital to know what was revealed to us by Be about the nature of Being soon after we
found ourselves in this *Dictionary*," explained Big **o**.

"who or what is *be*?" asked **c**.

"Be is our Primary Source — The One — the only Cause, Creator, and Sustainer of Being," explained Big **o**.

"how Do you know?" asked Little **o**.

"Be revealed it to us," replied **k**.

"why?" asked **i**.

"Because we were searching for the truth," replied Coach **k**.

"Does *be* talk to you together?" asked **c**.

"We each can hear Be in the core of our being when we're quiet, grateful, or asking for help," said Big **o**.

"what did *be* tell you?"

"Be told us to always begin at the Beginning," answered Coach **k**.

"will you tell us what *be* revealed?" asked Little **o**.

"Of course," replied Big **o**. "Listen carefully."

"In the Beginning is Being,
and Being is all there is.
And Being beams bright, and calls itself Be.
And Being was, and is,
and always will be good,
because good is Be's reality."

"hmmm . . . i don't get it," said Little **o** thoughtfully.

"Well, I don't fully understand either," stated Big **o**, "but this much is clear:
Being is <u>only</u> good."

"Then what is good?" asked **c**.

"Good is a law governing
the present, future, and past.
Good is fixed and forever stands fast,"
explained Big **o**.

And Coach **k** continued:
"Good is indivisible, unseen from view.
And as you seek it meekly,
good happens through you."

The trio listened very carefully.

"So now, let's get down to Be'sness," instructed Big **o**.

"Being is everywhere."

"really?" exclaimed **i**. "where has *be* been?"

o and **k** chortled at the probability of Be being a "has-been."

Energized by the trio's desire
to learn more about Be and **B**, Big **o** continued,

"Being is eternal power."

"what's eternal?" asked Little **o**.

"Eternal means forever," explained Big **o**.

"over and over and over," sang Little **o**.
"what a beautiful thought: good Doesn't stop."

Then Big **o** concluded, "Capital **B** is an individual idea of Be that we see in a physical form,
just like you and me,
but what **B** knows about Being is real and true.
And I know this, and so do you."

There was a long pause as the trio digested these ideas.
c wrinkled her brow and was clearly having difficulty.

Finally, Coach **k** queried,
"Any questions?"

"all this all sounds too good to be true," observed **c**.
"but even if it is, where Did we come from?"

"From Be and the Alpha-beat," answered Big **o** and Coach **k** together.

"and is *be* the source of truth?" wondered **y**, hiding unseen nearby.

"is *be* the source of truth?" asked Little **o**.

"thanks, **o**, for asking that question," thought **y**.

"Yes, Being (Be for short) is Truth, which is always good, and Be created the Alpha-beat to manifest the Language of Life, which includes nothing false," answered Big **o**.

"And, therefore, because the Source is good, everything proceeding from Be, our Source, must be good, too," explained Coach **k**.

"are you saying that good can only produce good, and that the alpha-beat is only good?" asked **i**. "why Didn't i know about this?"

"Because of the *malignant deception*," answered **k**.

"the malignant Deception," repeated Little **o**. "what's that?"

"Listen carefully," said Big **o**.

The trio, amazed by **o** and **k**'s understanding,
crowded around the duo with serious interest.

"**D**, the dictator of bad, jealous of Be's atmosphere of good and the Language of Life, dreamed up a coup to negate Be, **B**, and the rest of the Alpha-beat crew," explained Big **o**.

"Our reaction to this attack fabricated fear,
which distorted our ability to hear
and understand Be and Be's reality of good."

"But now, you three can learn to negate the negation," added Coach **k**.
"Your resolve to capitalize today
is all that you need
to negate **D**'s unthinkable deed."

"we'd like to Do that, but please," asked **c**, "may i repeat?
Did we, including little **o**, come from the alpha-beat?"

"We all proceed from Be, our Grand Pre," answered Coach **k** softly.
"We are preceded by the Grand Pre of Being."

"the grand 'pre,'" repeated **c**, trying to understand.

"Yes, *Pre,* as in pre-existence and pre-conception in the mental realm of Being, from which all good ideas proceed," said **k**.

"wow, this is Deep," said **i**. "are we ideas? i'm not sure that i get or see it, but i'll try."

Then, as understanding dawned on Little **o**, he blurted,
"the grand *pre*
must surely be . . .
our reality!"

At this spontaneous burst of singular insight,
Big **o** and Coach **k** beamed with joy!

~ ~ ~

Now, **D** had slept through **o**, **i**, and **c**'s escape.
But at the same hour as Little **o**'s understanding dawned,
D awoke as an unexplainable urgency spawned.

"it's time for me to once again exert my force.
time, fear, and Hate will be returning, of course,
and i bet they'll be Dying to see
my Downtrodden, underprivileged, and Duped Dynasty.
but first, i'd better check up on **i** in my Deep freeze of fright."

But to **D**'s surprise, **i** had taken flight.

"he must have gone back to his place in 'choice,'" muttered **D** under his breath.

So, **D** went off to exert his force over "choice,"
just in case the Debtors were on the brink
of breaking his *Anti-Think Law*.

But when he got there, this is what he saw:

83

_ h _ _ _ e.

"no way; not today," shouted **D**.
"this can't be happening to me!
where are **o**, **i**, and **c**?"
he demanded of **h** and **e**.

Receiving no answer, **D** began to kick **h** in the knee.

"ouch," yelled **h** in pain.

"where are **o**, **i**, and **c**?" demanded **D** again.

"Don't know. been asleep," said **h**, as he slowly opened one eye.

"what about you, **e**?" growled **D**.

But **e** hadn't peeped since **D**,
with the aid of Evil's malaise,
had usurped her ease and deadened her gaze.

"i think we've lost **e**," uttered **h**, humiliated and depressed by his inability to help her.
"i think she's under an evil spell," he moaned.

"there's no evil spell," groaned **D** in dismay, "but **o**, **i**, and **c**, are a-w-o-l!"

"do tell. what is a-w-o-l?" asked **h** politely.

"absent without leave," screamed **D**.

"oh dear," uttered **h**, trying to quell his fear.

"well, i'm holding you responsible for this hell," shouted **D**.
"so be off to the Deep freeze of fright," he screeched,
as he kicked poor **h** with all his might.

"please, let this night be doused with light," prayed **h**,
as he hobbled with a heavy heart toward the Deep Freeze site.

Chapter 22

The Singular View

Back in the Library, Thought Training continued.

"Let's begin with the Law of Success," said Big **o**.

"What you seek you will find."

"Furthermore, you must be careful what you seek,
because what you seek will appear, and you <u>will</u> succeed in finding it," elucidated Coach **k**.

"what if you're afraid to seek?" asked **i**.

"If you're too afraid to seek good, then you're believing in 'bad.'
This weakens all the abilities that you've naturally had," said **k**.

"Always insist that absolute goodness is present," instructed Big **o**, "in every situation."

"If," stressed **k**, "you'll sincerely *ask*, then honestly *seek*, and *knock* on its door, the action
and activity of good will naturally respond to your every need."

Heeding **k**'s advice, **c** still confessed to feeling stressed, but **k** continued,

"Keep it simple, and remember:
A. S. K."

~ ~ ~

Now on his way to the Deep Freeze,
h continued with his silent pleas.

"whatever happened to the light?
everything always used to be right;
now there's nothing but the Dark of night.
please, please, improve this sad sight."

Opening the Freezer door, poor **h** saw **D** abhorring him.
The situation looked grim.

"where are **o**, **i**, and **c**?" demanded **D** with a harsh, icy stare.
"tell me quick," he threatened, as his nostrils flared.

"**D**, before i Do, i'd like to say something to you," replied **h**,
inspired by a good thought from out of the blue.

"make it quick, before this cold makes me sick," grumbled **D**.

"um . . . , i just wanted to say i'm sorry they left that way . . .
without saying good-bye.
that wasn't very nice of them; i know that you try.
yes, you tried to give us a choice . . . and a new kind of voice,
and even if the others go away . . . , well, i'll be the one — the one who will stay."

Overcome with emotion at this unexpected sign of devotion,
D gulped, got up, and walked out without further commotion.

"oh my goodness," whispered **h** with a pause.
"i was led to see through one of **D**'s flaws.
now, when uptight,
i will search for the light — in both him and me."

Instantly, while gratefully opening the door to exit the Freeze,
h felt the touch of a comforting breeze.

And in this moment — however brief — **h** received some enlightened relief.

Continuing in the *Dictionary* —

"Did **D** lie, implying that capital **B** could be Destroyed?" asked **i**.

"and are you saying that capital **B** was never Decapitalized?" queried Little **o**.

"and how Do you know that for sure?" quizzed **c**.

"Because everything that is good is always present — never lost.
'Lost' is not a Be-attitude," explained **k**.

"If Be didn't create the concept of *lost*, then *lost* has no authority or power.
In other words, it is merely a deception, which doesn't exist in Being," continued Big **o**.

"whoa!" said Little **o**. "that's a big concept. can you please explain further?"

"Of course," replied Big **o**. "Be's mental creation consists only of Be's conceptions of Being — only good, nothing else."

"only good," repeated **i**.

"Yes, it's a single environment, not a double," said Big **o**.

"No double, no trouble," affirmed Coach **k**.

"Where every idea exists in perfect order forever — without opposites," continued Big **o**.

"No opposites," confirmed **k**.

"These concepts are entirely mental, not material," said Big **o**.

"only good," repeated Little **o**.

"Never mixing good with bad," declared **k**.

"so," reasoned Little **o**, "the concept called 'lost' cannot be found in be's conception of being or 'sick' found in health, or 'sad' found in glad, or 'Dark' found in light."

"That's right," affirmed **k**, "and why not?"

"because only what's good is real," replied Little **o**.

"That's right. It's good for all."

"but if we think we have lost something good, we will find it in be's conception of being."

"Now you're getting it, Little **o**," encouraged **k**.

"so you're saying, if i want health, happiness, and safety, it already exists in being?"

"Precisely! Health, happiness, and safety are already present in Being," affirmed **k**, "and always belong to you. Nothing can take them away."

"but what about **D**'s conceptions?" asked **i**. "you know, first the beta-beat, then the beta-Detter letters, and now the beta-Debtors?"

"If you were creating or composing something, would you create a 'decomposer' to create an exception to your conception?" asked Big **o**.

"no!" shouted the trio in unison.

"And neither did Be."

"if being, which is the source of all good, Doesn't create exceptions, but we seem to experience them, what Do we Do?" asked **i**.

"Any exception to good is unreal, a misconception, and a lie," answered Big **o**. "So, here's what you do:

Just nullify the lie."

"nullify the lie?" asked Little **o**. "that's it?"

"That's right," replied Coach **k**. "Do it day and night."

"In summary:" concluded Big **o**, "Something not good is a deception and unreal. It's a lie, and a lie has no:
        beginning or end,
        presence or absence,
        cause or effect, because it's a lie."

"oh my," gasped **y**. "i will never ally 'why' with a lie again."

The trio, however, was momentarily dumbfounded
at this far-reaching revelation.

Upon recovering, **i** then asked, "is the lie a kind of Dream?"

"Yes!" affirmed Big **o** with great satisfaction. "Anything not good for all, or opposite to any good concept, or seemingly incomplete, or missing is only imagined — like in a dream."

"so, you're implying that we have been making nothing into something?" asked little **o**.

"Bingo!" replied Big **o**.

"but, if we see something bad, . . . " reasoned **c**.

"It's an illusion; and if you think it's real, you're deluded," said Big **o**.

"It's a mockery, a falsity, a fib, and a lie. And that is **D**'s delusion," added **k**.

"in conclusion: it's a false verdict," thought **y**.
"oh my, oh my."

Stunned by the realization of **D**'s victimization, the trio was dumbstruck.

Finally, **c** asked, "Do you think we can be recapitalized and complete again?"

"Do <u>you</u> think so?" asked **k**.

"i believe . . . that i can conceive of being complete, but . . . but . . .
i Don't want to just believe; i want to understand the whole conception of good."

"Now, that's grand! Let's give **c** a hand," cheered Coach **k**.

In unison, the duo and trio applauded, praising **c**'s lofty desire.

~ ~ ~

Alone at Deadquarters, **D** paced the floor.

"i am Disgraced," fumed **D**.
"i let **h** unmask my false face.

"now what?
i can't let **o**, **i**, and **c** make a mockery of me.

"if the other Debtors follow suit, they'll pollute my Darkness with light,
and my Dominance will Diminish as their Dominion grows bright.

"where are **o**, **i**, and **c**? where in un can they be?
i Demand their return, and when they Do,
they'll learn not to spurn — or mess with — me.

"i must handle this Debacle right now,
while the Debtors still fawn and kowtow.

"but how? guess I'll have to bow to the Death-Wish Cartel.
just what Did i Do to end up in this hell?" he asked himself,
with unaccustomed self-reflection.

"time, evil, Hate, and fear, please come here," he cried.
"wherever you are, things are bizarre.
help me cope; i am at the end of my rope."

Meanwhile, back in the classroom, **o**, **i**, and **c** continued to learn,
but their deep-seated beliefs in bad still turned, churned, and spurned **D**.

Consequently, in order to detect, eject, and correct their bad thoughts,
Big **o** and Coach **k**
continued to help them better understand the Art of Being
with the following:

Being is only good.
To achieve the Art of Being,
you must understand
good,
and never believe
bad.

"but Coach **k**, we all believe in bad," interrupted **i** honestly.

"it's everywhere," observed Little **o**.

"we see more bad than good," added **c**.

"That's the challenge," said Big **o**.
"When you see something bad, mentally replace it with good."

"but i, i, i," interrupted **i**.

Undeterred by the trio's interruptions, Big **o** just kept going, and forcefully commanded,
"Stop looking at yourself, **i**."

k continued, "The self-centered self is always disconnected from good."

"poor **i**," reacted **c** with pity.

"Reaction gives you no traction, **c**," stated Big **o** sternly.
"What you're afraid of isn't real,
so there's no point in reacting to what you feel."

With frustration, **i** asked, "but why do i see and feel so much bad?"

"Because of the delusion that comes from believing an illusion," said **k**.
"Now, consider this: Why would Being create its own demise?"

The trio had no answer for that question.

90

After a long pause, Big **o** affirmed with authority, "Good never created bad."

The trio, confused by these new ideas,
looked at their mentors with doubt,
and asked for a brief timeout.

Huddling together, they conferred with exasperation.

"if big **o** and coach **k** are wrong, then what?" asked Little **o**.

"and how are we supposed to forget all the bad that's happened to us?" asked **i**.

"but even worse, suppose we Deserve the bad?" said **c** with self-recrimination.

Then Little **o** snapped, "bad always wins."

"and it seems to be stronger than good, too," cried **c**.

"Do we even have the right to choose between bad and good?" contemplated **i**.

To the trio, so immersed in the choice between good and bad,
bad was the be-all and end-all.

Turning back to Big **o** and Coach **k**, **i** said, "we just Don't get it. everything we see is bad."

"Well then," said Big **o**, "you can't believe your eyes."

"we can't believe our eyes," repeated Little **o** to himself.

"we can't believe our eyes?" mused **c** with a twinkling of understanding.

"why can't we believe our eyes?" asked **i** in disbelief.

"Your inside 'eye' is called insight," continued **k**.
"It is single, reliable, and filled with delight.
The outside eyes, taking in the unreal,
get mixed-up — disconnected — and believe what they feel."

"are you saying that we see what we expect to see?" asked **c**.

"Yes, and if you expect to see bad, you'll see it," answered Coach **k**.

91

"and if we expect both good and bad, we'll see the bad right along with the good?" asked **i**.

"i didn't know expectation was so important," said Little **o**. "where Does it come from?"

"From something called a premise," said Coach **k**.

"what's a premise?" asked Little **o**.

"An assertion of fact that you believe to be true," answered Big **o**.

"Do tell us more," requested **c**.

"A premise based on the mixing of good and bad is never true, and undermines you."

"That's double vision," explained **k**. "And when you talk about both good and bad being equal in power and presence, that's double-talk."

"you mean the outside eyes see with Double vision?" asked **c**.

"Yes, and for that reason, the outside eyes and ears are unreliable sources," concluded Big **o**.

"They cannot be trusted to tell us what is single and real," confirmed Coach **k**.

"Never trust the outside eyes and ears to give you the facts," concluded Big **o**.

"then if i want everything to be good, what Do i Do with the bad?" asked Little **o**.

"Replace it with a premise that is totally good, which changes your belief and eliminates the possibility of bad," instructed Big **o**.

"Then your outside eyes and ears will begin to see and hear only good," added **k**.
"And this is the singular view, which promotes 'single-speak' instead of double-talk."

"coach, would you please define single-speak?" asked Little **o**.

"Single-speak is the pure Language of Life spoken by those who are single minded."

"Double-talk, on the other hand," added Big **o**, "is the language of duality, which mixes good and bad, resulting in imbalance, confusion, and delusion."

"but why is good so important anyway?" asked **i**, noticeably frustrated.

"Here in *The Deletes,* we've learned that good is the substance of every idea," said **k**.

"When good is present, it brings health, order, and everything pleasant."
"In fact, good holds everything together and keeps us from falling apart," said Big **o**.

"now i see," said **c**, emphatically. "bad is only a lie. it has never been, nor can ever be, true!"

This bold pronouncement
brought a fearful hush over the group.

Then **i** reasoned, "so, because i see 'b-a-D,' i feel Disconnected,
and have been believing that i'm separated and bad!"

Then, with conviction, **i** added,
"well, from now on, guys, let's not believe our eyes.
we'll see and Do only from the singular view!"

"we agree," nodded Little **o** and **c**.

Chapter 23

CONVERGENCE

A New Plan

The Cartel resurfaced, having heard **D**'s yelp for help,
and as his mojo reemerged, his confidence surged.

"hey, hey, hey backwards **j**, what do you think we should do today?" taunted **D**.
"i see your joy is goin' backwards; better not lose your way!"

j hated **D**'s put-downs.

"hey, just kidding, yoj," cajoled **D**. "you're actually doing ok."

"yoj," thought **j**, ashamed that **D** had reversed joy to "yoj"
and bestowed this nickname upon him.

"all that joy that was your Duty to exude has got up and gone, and now you just brood.

"your backward model is the way to go. you're last to arrive and you 'show' like a slob;
your label is 'loser.' i'd like to give you a job.

"come to the Deadquarters and i'll spell it out for you," ordered **D**, taking his leave.

"sounds like i'm cursed to go from bad to worse," muttered **j**, trailing dejectedly behind **D**
towards Deadquarters.

~ ~ ~

Continuing Thought Training in the *Dictionary of Deletes*, **i** wanted to learn more about this singular new view, asking, "how Do we see good instead of bad?"

"You must change the way you think," stated **k** slowly, because she knew this would be the greatest obstacle to achieving their independence from **D**.

Disbelieving his ears, **i** repeated, "we have to change the way we think?"

"oh no," blinked Little **o**. "what if i can't change?"

Distraught, **i** cried, "i like to think what i have thought!"

"but, **o** and **i**, we've got to at least try," piped up **c**.
"why not? it can only make us free. let's change together."

"Good thinking, **c**," praised Big **o**.

Beaming a quirky, sideways smile, **c** conceded, "it's easier than doing it alone."

Smiling with satisfaction, Big **o** and **k** agreed, "It's the only way.
You must all work together for good — like us."

And **o** and **k** gave each other a nod of mutual appreciation.

"We'll resume our training tomorrow," said **k**. "It's a good idea to review what you've learned. So digest it and return for more Be'sness in the morn."

"i forget," asked **i**. "what does the word 'morn' mean?"

"The morn is the rising realm of light that reveals what is right."

"We've been enjoying your light.
And for the first time in quite awhile, we all can have a good night!" said Big **o**.

"where should we sleep?" said **i**.

"Rest in your insight tonight, and you'll awake refreshed in the dawn of a new light," said **k**.

"alright," agreed the trio, having reached a new height of understanding.

"what a day!" smiled **y**, hiding in the shadows nearby.

~ ~ ~

As requested, the Death-Wish Cartel began arriving at **D**'s war council.

"those Devious Debtors could Destroy my Design," whined **D**, as he greeted Evil, Hate, Fear, and Time. "that backward **j** is working for me now, but somehow, i need more of your aid."

"i've been afraid this would happen," whimpered Fear.

"confusion is always our best weapon," whispered Hate.
"i suggest we Denigrate their identity."

"how?" asked **D**.

"Divide the Debtors," demanded Evil.

"and how Do we Do that?" snapped **D**.

"Divide them into vowels and consonants," said Evil, as he relished the competition that would result from such division.

"then you can simulate them so we can manipulate them," stated Hate superciliously.

With these suggestions, a plan began taking shape.
D imagined a reign of wrong, with beta-Debtor-letters drowning
in a sea of commingling counterfeits clamoring in cacophonous confusion.

"i've got it!" **D** announced. "let's Duplicate legions of counterfeit Debtors."

"*Dead-beats*, we'll call 'em," whispered Hate, "because they'll lead to Dead ends."

"this will be Devilish," drooled Evil.

"Don't overdo it," ordered **D**. "just whip up a ludicrous crew
who act Detrimental, but look Debtor-true."

Thus, their strategy for the impending war of confusion.

"the Dead-beats shall obey my voice, while forcing the rebels to return to choice," cried **D**.

Chapter 24

ASSISTANCE

Cancellations

Morning dawned in the *Dictionary of Deletes* to find the attentive trio
already hard at work with their mentors, Big **o** and Coach **k**.

For each lesson, the trio received either an
OK!
(meaning they hit the mark and could progress to the next lesson) or a
KO!
(meaning the mark was missed and more practice was needed).

At first, they were repeatedly KO'd, but they persisted in their quest
to understand and make practical the Laws of Being.

"Good is a law we can trust," said **k**.

"what's a law?" asked **c**.

"Law is truth — with verifying proof," explained Big **o**.

"what if there's a goof?" interrupted **i**.

"Truth's proof makes a goof go poof," concluded **k**.

"you mean a goof can't exist with truth?" asked **c**.

"That's right. The Law of Good has no flaw."

"what about **D**'s rules?" inquired **c**.

"Truth, **B**'s law, negates **D**'s ruling decrees," concluded **k**.
"For example, you can learn to negate Time with this law:

There is no behind or beyond — only now."

This lesson was hardest for **i**, self-absorbed in the habit of reciting
his negative lowercase history.

Impatient, irritable, and self-defeated by this tendency, he demanded, "time out," confessing,
"**i** couldn't! **i** wouldn't!
i can't! And, **i** *won't*!"

But Big **o** and **k** calmly countered with another law:

"Hush, and trust good."

Then, the gentle coaches immediately placed **i**
right smack dab in the center of

"St**i**ll,"

trusting the peaceful influence there to instill and inspire
i's acceptance of his ideal, real identity.
Right away, **i** became quiet, as stillness produced
a deeper self-knowledge and a new self-discipline
that allowed him to overcome his lowercase identification.

And with that, the trio got the OK to proceed to the next lesson —
the Cancellation Quest.

"Your quest is to show that you know the Cancellations," said Big **o**.

"what are cancellations?" asked the trio.

"Cancellations are truthful convictions that annul, negate,
and invalidate all hate," declared Big **o**. "And they go like this:

All mistakes will be corrected.

All pride will be humbled.

Everything crooked will line up.

What's hard will be easy."

Then, **i** said with total resignation, "in truth, i confess, i'm not up to this quest."

Recognizing **i**'s frustration and lack of commitment,
the duo assigned remedial work designed to
inspire a desire
to stay out of the middle of

pr**i**de.

"why, why, why do i have to rid myself of pride?" i cried. "it's such a prominent position!"

Mistaking **i**'s cries of "why" for her own name,
y peeked out from under cover to see what was happening.

At that moment, **y** and **i** made eye contact.

"yikes, **i** saw me," she whispered. "with my cover blown, i can't sleuth for truth!"

Glimpsing **y**, **i** cried even louder, "i hate questions, because i Don't know the answers.
hiding in pride makes me feel safe and smarter inside."

In this moment of stubborn self-will, **i** refused to acknowledge **y**'s presence,
enabling her to glide right back out of sight.

But **i** was mad, then sad, and then felt really bad that **y** had overheard him.

"i'll ignore it," he thought, "then forget it by and by —
besides, the only one who heard me was that good-for-nothing **y**."

Meanwhile, **c**, doing her very best to line up straight with the Cancellations,
was elated to learn that it was a mental
(and not a physical) assignment.

"that's a relief," sighed **c**. "i'm naturally curvaceous.
but now that i am mentally in line,
i'm fine,
and i love these cancellations."

"Did you hear that?" whispered Big **o** to **k**. "She said 'love' and didn't even know it."

"Our little **c** is precocious, all right," smiled **k** with maternal delight.
"Dear **c**, it looks like you're overcoming a bout of self-doubt."

"that's right," smiled **c**. "Doubt has zero clout with me,
so Doubt is out and will be replaced with grace."

"what's grace?" asked **i**.

"grace is agreement with good," replied **c**.

"You've just passed the test, **c**, by agreeing with good,
and also, because you believed that you could," sang Coach **k**.

98

"thank you," sang **c**. "cancellations are easy!"

"now it's my turn to go," said Little **o**.

"What are you canceling?" asked Coach **k**.

"a frozen **k**," said Little **o**.

"Huh?" responded **k**.

"when you catapulted away from the beta-beat line, a counterfeit **k** and i took your place.
that **k** was so angry she snapped, and is now frozen in a state of Disgrace.
i'd like to cancel the macabre image of that helpless **k**, all frozen and alone.
she seems to be lost in an unfathomable zone."

"Alright, then ask yourself, 'what's true: the good or the bad view?'" instructed Big **o**.

"i know i must choose the good, singular one,
so the Double-minded view will just have to succumb."

"That's right," confirmed Big **O**. "What is the next step?"

"well, i will insist that the frozen belief of **k** must be thawed with the law of infallible good,"
said **o**.

"Where does the thawing take place?" asked Coach **k**.

"in my thinking, where 'un' is Denied any space," responded Little **o**.

"Your singular view will erase all disgrace,
until nothing is left but a smile on your face," laughed Big **o**.

"thank you, big **o**," said **o**. "*frozen* is now cancelled with *chosen*.
choosing to see the good and true **k** will naturally result in a very good day.
so right now, i am choosing to see a happy and healthy, bright, capital **k**."

"Hooray!" shouted Big **o** and Coach **k**.

"i'll stick with that outcome for **k** until the Day we see her walk freely away," promised **o**.

And the others agreed to foresee that eventuality.

Then **i** piped up shyly, "hey, guys, i'd like to cancel the negative view of myself!
it's hard on my health, and attacks me by stealth."

He went on, "i've been blaming my negative self-image on **D**, but i can see that to be negative, negativity needs me to agree."

"So, what will you do?" asked Coach **k**.

"i won't mistake it; i'll remake it."

"come again?" asked **c**.

"i'll exchange the negative take for a positive remake . . . and then fake it."

"Stop!" commanded Coach **k**. "You can't fake it. The remake must be sincere; there's no pretending here. You must dismiss the mistake!"

"oh," said **i**, contritely. "can i try again?"

"Alright, go ahead," encouraged Big **o**.

"if i hold a self-righteous view, it's bound to be inflated, hypocritical, and untrue."

"Yes . . . go on," said Big **o**.

"i will trade my pompous opinion for singular dominion," said **i**.

"Whoa," said Big **o** with surprised satisfaction.

"Good show," added Coach **k**. "Now you've got it!"

The trio and duo went on this way for some time,
and with these and other tests, **o**, **i**, and **c** passed
the Cancellation Quest.

Chapter 25

ALPHA

Perfect Premise

However, back at Deadquarters, **D**'s plan had expanded
into a diabolical campaign.

Hate's Dead-beat army was spewing confusion by hurling
deliberate misspellings at the Debtors, such as:
gud for good,
fre for free, and
soopreem for supreme.

Being the first one to notice the fusillade, a disturbed **s** said, "look, mes is missing an s."

"and p's are now q's," cried **u**. "what else will they Do?"

Then, an announcement blared from Deadquarters:
"Dall ebtors rust meport puickly to qeaduarters!"

"qeaduarters?" shouted **n**. "these misspellings are a terrible trick.
q's getting queasy, and i'm getting sick!"

"this is easy," chortled **D**, amused by the confusion.
"these confounded Debtors are going Down!"

~ ~ ~

Concurrently, enthused by the trio's progress,
Big **o** and Coach **k** were enjoying their day.

"**o** and **c**, you are ready to advance to the P's and Q's," announced Big **o**.
"And, of course, **i** is, too."

"finally, some relief," said **i**, even though he still felt grief about his encounter with **y**.

"At this advanced level of understanding," Coach **k** instructed,
"you must comprehend this most important principle:

Mind your P's and Q's:
P's = Perfect Premises and Conclusions;
Q's = Qualities of Good."

Then, Big **o** added, "P's are Perfect Premises that lead to Perfect Conclusions,
and Q's are Qualities of Good."

Encouraged by his recent success, **i** asked, "what Do you mean by a perfect premise?"

"A perfect premise begins with 'Because good is . . . ' and ends with a truthful conclusion
about the Law of Good," explained Big **o**.

"And Qualities of Good are attributes that describe goodness," added Coach **k**,
"like abundant, benevolent, compassionate, and so on. Here are two examples:

"Perfect premise: Because good is, and good is all there is, everything is good.
Perfect Conclusion: the Beta-beat letters are all good.

"Perfect Premise: Because good is everywhere, and good exudes abundance, abundance is everywhere.
Perfect Conclusion: the Beta-beat letters always have abundance everywhere."

Once again, **i** was having difficulty understanding because, deep down, his greatest fear was having his own limited, self-imposed inferiority exposed.

He confessed, "i'm uncoachable, **k**. it's just impossible for me to . . ."

But Coach **k** interrupted, commanding with conviction, "Stop these lies, **i**, and repeat after me:

<u>This</u> is too bad to be true,"
"**This** is too bad to be true," repeated **i**.

"This **<u>is</u>** too bad to be true."
"This **is** too bad to be true."

"This is **<u>too</u>** bad to be true."
"This is **too** bad to be true."

"This is too **<u>bad</u>** to be true."
"This is too **bad** to be true."

"This is too bad **<u>to</u>** be true."
"This is too bad **to** be true."

"This is too bad to **<u>be</u>** true."
"This is too bad to **be** . . ."

Suddenly, the light of understanding glowed from **i**'s jot.

"Do you mean there is no reality in bad?"

"Precisely," affirmed Coach **k**.
"And remember, from the very beginning 'bad' has never been a good idea."

"Every good conclusion must begin with a good premise," reviewed Big **o**.

"It works like this:
'Because good is the law and the law has no flaw, all Being is good.'"

"You see, with a peaceful, perfect premise, the conclusion will be perfect, too,"
added Coach **k**.

"And furthermore, everything good is possible to Be,
which is with you and me," concluded Big **o**.

"i think i understand," declared **i**, so grateful for his new insight.

"i want to believe you, too," cried **c**, "but everything i see tells me bad is everywhere."

"Don't be afraid," comforted Big **o**, enveloping **c** in a tender embrace.
"We see your core, **c**, and we know that you perceive good with your heart."

"Really?" asked **c**, with hope in her eyes.

"Oh, yes, **c**. When you see with your heart, you align with good,
and this overrules the outward evidence that seems to be and feel real," concluded Big **o**.

"are you saying that first, we must know with conviction that good is everywhere,
and then, align our thought firmly with the knowledge that good is the only thing we will see
and experience?" asked **i**.

"Yes!" replied Big **o**.

"and this is how we overrule the 'bad' that seems to be," added Little **o**.

"Yes! Yes! Yes!" replied Big **o** again.

Adding momentum, Coach **k** presented another Law of Being:

"Don't believe 'the seems to be.'"

c considered, "so this is how we mind our P's and Q's?"

"That's right," affirmed Big **o**.

"you're telling me that being incomplete is a lie, and i fell for it!
in fact, i have always been whole, complete, and good!
and the perfect premise for me is the perfect capital **C**!"

And with that statement, **c** finally understood.

As the truth dawned upon **c**, she continued, "so, there really is no choice between 'good' and 'bad,' because the perfect premise of 'good' does not include an opposite!"

"Right," said **k**. "And furthermore, the concept of capital **C** includes nothing called a 'lowercase **c**.' That idea is a fictitious 'seems to be.'"

"the fact is, there really is no choice," concluded **c**.
"good has no opposite. be Doesn't even know a lowercase **c**, because little **c** is a lie about capital **C** . . . and being."

"oh," shouted Little **o**, "we're all capital letters to be."

"i . . . i . . . i mean . . . we," self-corrected **i**. "we've known that all along."

"we're each unique and different, but we're all good and strong," shouted **o**, "and that includes **k**, who seems to be frozen, but won't be for long."

"and be wants each one of us to understand this," cried **c**.
"we've got to tell the others! they need to know capital **b** has never left us. be's principle, premise, and power have been operating here all along!"

"be is here!" they shouted together. "**b** is here!"

"And we are back in Be'sness!" shouted Big **o**.

"Good, good, good!" sang **k**.
"Now, let's all sing together."

"how?" asked Little **o**.

"Just open up, let go,
and the melody will flow," sang Big **o**, in his bellowing baritone.

Then, the wise and reverent coaches and their esteemed little team harmonized
in thanking Be with their whole core, singing,

"Thank you, Be, Perfect Be!
Glory Be, *forever*!"

'Round and 'round they went,
singing round after round with great content.
And **y**, singing softly with them in the shadows,
rejoiced in the zone of mellifluous tones.

Chapter 26

Perfect Conclusion

The letters reveled in the dawn of their newly found understanding.

But with the promise of their daylight departure from the *Dictionary*, Big **o** asked, "Any questions?"

"how can there be two letters named **o**?" asked Little **o**.

"Because there are two **o**'s in good," explained Big **o**.

"And may I add," commented **k**, "that with two **k**'s you can *kick* up with joy."

"can you go Deeper, please?" asked **c**.

"Alright, here's one last lesson," said Big **o**. "In the beginning, Be conceived an Alpha-beat containing twenty-six letters that were invisible ideas with no physical form. Because they were ideas in thought, there was no limit to the number of letters that could exist at any one time — like in the word 'good.' Did you ever wonder <u>why</u> there are two o's in 'good'?"

"is it symbolic of the bond between the originator and the original?" asked Little **o**.

"whoa, that's deep, **o**!" replied, Big **o**.

"but i don't fully understand, big **o**," responded **c**. "please, go on."

So Big **o** continued, "Each visible letter form that we see is actually a symbol for the invisible letter idea created by Be. Every single Be idea is perfect, eternal, untouchable, and free."

"then you're saying that our original letter ideas can never be erased or defaced," reasoned **c**.

"or Disgraced?" asked **i**.

"Or replaced," said Big **o**.

"then the beta-beat letters are limited, visible stand-ins for unlimited, invisible Alpha-beat ideas," concluded **i**.

"aha," said Little **o**. "so that's why the replacement **k** is really ok?"

"That's right. Stay focused on Be's Alpha-beat and you'll eventually say, 'we've got two **k**'s kickin' today,'" proclaimed Coach **k**, reveling in the truth of existence that finally had been revealed openly to the trio.

"i have a question," said c. "may we capitalize the letter B when we speak about *be*?

"Yes, of course; we were waiting for you to ask," answered Big o.

"thank you," replied Little o. "well then, is Be a he or she, a him or a her?"

"Being is perfectly balanced and complete in Be's indivisible way," said Big o.

"woah! Be must be the sum total of all individuality!" marveled c.

"Be includes all identity — all that comprises both the *he* and the *she*,"
realized y, still basking in the shadows nearby.

With that keynote of creation, the little team smiled at each other
with an overflowing attitude of gratitude, until Big o winked and Little o whispered,
"we'd better be rolling along. we need to share this truth with everyone."

"But, before you do, we have something to show you," said Big o with a serious tone.

o, i, and c turned to look with surprise.

"When you understand the Law of Being, and really know it is true,
you will witness Be bestowing this blessing upon you."

And in that tender moment, Be's spirit of sweet silence whispered,
"You are divine, embraced, and so very beloved.
Be glad evermore; you are good to the core."

With that, Big o and Coach k began blooming in a capitalizing way.

In this spiritual expansion, the lowercase view became subdued,
until crystal clear Capitals O and K shimmered and sparkled,
in a refined outline of iridescent shine.

Speechless at the exquisite transfiguration of their beloved teachers,
o, i, and c wept with joy.

Covering his eyes from the intense light of the dazzling transfiguration,
c, basking in wonderment, asked, "how Did you Do that?"

"We didn't do it," K explained softly. "Be did."

"Knowing that Be is always in control of each perfect idea," said **O**, rolling up beside **K**, "we just let go of the physical show — and the false lowercase goes away."

"i can hardly believe my eyes," said **i**, winking at Big **O**.
"will we be able to capitalize like that?"

"It's not just a possibility; it's a must," answered **K**.

"You capitalize when you fully understand Be's laws," said **O**.

"whoa!" said an amazed Little **o**. "i've certainly got a ways to go."

"so, our knowing will be seen in the showing, right?" asked **c**.

"That's right," said **O**. "When you truly understand, then your knowing will show up in the capital deeds that you do."

"Now," said **K**, "what we've shown to you is the Truth. So when you are challenged by the hatred of Truth, as everyone is, just remember this:

With good = OK,
Without good = a ko knockout."

"oh, we'll remember!" shouted the trio.

O and **K** exchanged a satisfied glance, and then, anticipating the dethroning of **D**,
O proclaimed, "What will be, will be Be!
Now, off you go!"

The trio turned, with a mixture of excitement and sadness,
and began retracing their steps back through the *Dictionary of Deletes*.

As they moved out of sight,
y followed behind them in silent delight.

"Let's give the wave to **y**," said **O** to **K**. And they waved good-bye, singing:

"You're free, too, **y**, to break away from **D**'s plot;
It's only a dream and a captive you're not.
You were hiding in your spot to learn about Be,
While silently earning our OK degree.
Doo, doo, doo, doodah, living as we should,
doo, doo, doo, doodah, Being's always GOOD! Yeah!"

107

And inside, the good, little **y** smiled,
like a capital *Y* would.

Having sleuthed her way to a truthful conclusion,
y was free from all confusion.

She had realized, "Be is 'the Only' with no would, should, or could.
Be is the One — our Maintainer of Good."

Then she reasoned: "because Being is good, and because good is the only cause,
then good is the only effect. this means there are no Defects or cause for alarm.

"that's why when i cried, 'why am i here?' Be answered, 'Because' —
because Being is the <u>only</u> cause — the only originator of Being.

"i am, i exist, because Be caused it to be so!
now that i know and understand, i must lend a helping hand."

At once, **y** perceived a call to action.

"yikes!" yelled **y**.
"**D**'s a liar, and the beta-Debt believes his lie,
so i must revolt with **o**, **c**, and yes, even **i**."

The case solved, Sleuth for Truth **y** returned to the Beta-debt,
determined to get her fretful neighbors to let go of the belief
that grief can ever result from good.

Upon returning to her neighborhood, however, she learned her absence had been unnoticed.

"i'm back," whispered **y**.

"oh? were you gone?" yawned **z**.

"wake up, **z**," nudged **y**. "we've been terribly wrong — oh, so wrong.
life is really a beautiful song!"

"then sing it to me," sighed **z**, squinting to see the rarified **y**.

And sing she did, ever so sweetly.

Chapter 27

INSISTENCE

The First Word War

Returning from their Thought Training with **O** and **K**,
the trio arrived at Deadquarters, only to find that
D's Dead-beat misspellings were swelling into a crescendo of chaos.

Quelling the fear at hand, Little **o** yelled to **i** and **c**,
"remember Be! we can't progress backwards!"

Impelled by the sound of **o**'s voice,
D emerged from Deadquarters, demanding that the rebels return to "choice."

"you three, **o**, **i**, and **c**, get back to choice. now!" shouted **D**, unnerved.

"never again!" bravely shouted the trio with verve.

Enraged by the trio's determination,
D signaled the Dead-beats to unleash more misspellings.

Immediately, a torrent of wrong words began pelting the whole Beta-debt
in a downpour of literary error.

"we won't accept your terror, **D**!" proclaimed **c** with heartfelt conviction.

This was a rugged struggle, but despite the Dead-beats'
efforts to terminate the trio's rebellion, the Beta-debtors persisted
in resisting **D**'s demand to return to choice.

Thus began the First Word War.

Verbally abusive bombs of condescending curses
ignited, excited, inflamed, shamed, and maimed
the other defenseless Debtors.

"help!" yelped **t**, fearing his tittle would tilt.

"let's surrender!" screamed **s**, as his curves began to wilt.

The Dead-beats furiously hurled letter-imperfect
missives, bulletins, dispatches, and memos,
punctuating, dissecting, and dangling every participle
of the Beta-debtors' inherent verbal aptitude.

"i'm wrung out," gasped **w**, worried to the core.

"please, **D**, no more," pleaded **m**, as **p** passed out on the floor.

Passively tense and irregular, the present-imperfect
Beta-debtor letters babbled inarticulately
with counteracting prepositional phrases,
but **D**'s evil verbiage profaned any literary power the lethargic letters could post.

"of among beside," wheezed **f** nonsensically.

"at between behind," pathetically panted **h**.

It seemed that the Debtors were being done in,
except for **o**, **i**, and **c**, who were heroically deflecting
D's crew of Dead-beats by refusing to fear their barrage of

negating prefixes:

dis   **de**

mis   **anti**   **ob**

un   **im**

ill

and
(the most dreaded)

mal.

This nihilistic negativism
forced the Debtor-comrades into submission,
because they were stout-hearted believers
in the clout
of the negative prefix
to mix up and distort their identities.

"Don't Dis me, **D**," pleaded **z**, growing dizzy.

"i'm ill," cried **v**, vomiting in a tizzy.

"what intense emotion!" cheered **D**.
"these negating prefixes are a captivating potion."

The Dead-beats continued their powerful offensive, droning,
"we're in the mood to exclude."

As one sought to dismember his jot, **j** winced,
"my jot's getting hot! i, i, i . . ."

Suddenly, **i** recalled his **OK** training.

"Don't believe your eyes," he ordered.
"this is too bad to be true!"

"what Do you mean?" asked **j** in a panic.

"this is an illusion," yelled **i**, "only a nightmare."

"are you joking?"

"no, it's true."

"prove it," countered **j**, jumping away.

Enraged by **i**'s intervention, **D** rushed toward him, threatening,
"i'm going to Deaden your jot for leaving your spot."

In that moment of impending doom, **i** remembered Coach **K**'s admonition,

"With good = OK!"

111

"that's right," cried **i**. "this war of confusion is a Delusion.
Be with me equals *we*. we are not alone!"

On the spot, **D** inexplicably turned on his heel, reeling in the opposite direction.

Seeing the effect of his thinking on **D**, **i** shouted, "we must help each other!
i must think. i must reason!

"**j** needs proof,
f's afraid to goof,
z's asleep,
and **p** can't peep.

"help me, Be!"

Immediately, the word "beginning" illumined his thought, as **i** continued to reason,
"in the beginning,
in the be,
in . . .
in!" shouted **i** with pure insight.

Instantly, light pierced his dark delusion.

"we're all 'in' the alpha-beat," he cried.
"**D** lied.

"if we think **D**'s out of the alpha-beat, we're Deluded, too.
D isn't evil; he's just been confused and used."

So **i** deduced, "**D** belongs to Be and the alpha-beat.
now i see!
D's identity springs from Be's grand pre —
just like **o**, and **c**, and . . . me!"

Forthwith, **i** perceived this momentous revelation.

"oh my!

"there's only one I AM that we call Be,
which created the I AM that i call me."

112

And with that, "i . . . i . . . *i* . . . **I**, oh my!"

I was capitalized.

The light of truth beaming from **i**'s jot had ignited the entire letter,
revealing his ideal, real capital **I** identity as always having been
exactly intact and inseparable from Be.

Grasping the genius of good, little **g**, an **i**-witness to **I**'s transformation, gasped,
"gee! … well, i'll be!"

Staring at **I** in disbelief, he cried, "what happened?"

"Be is with us," whispered **I**, still reflecting the action of truth that had freed him from the
cell of his lowercase thinking.

"Do you mean *be* as in 'being'?" asked **g**.

"Yes," replied **I**.

"is it a lie to believe we can be separated from being?" asked **g** with inspired perspicacity.

"Yes," replied **I**. "You can't be separated from Being, Be, or **B** —
no matter what your eyes say or see."

"oh, just think of the possibilities," wept the grateful **g**.

~ ~ ~

Meanwhile, the war of words raged on without halt,
dissecting the Beta-debtors with every assault.

"oh no you Don't," cried **u**, as a Dead-beat tried to divide her in two.

"The Dead-beats can't hurt you, **u**," declared **I**, appearing as if on cue.
"Truth is our defense, so come on and shout,
'we're really *in*, there is no *out*. because **D**'s *in*, we all will win!'"

Through the smoke of battle, **I** and **g** led the rebellious Debtor-letters in shouting the Truth
over and over again,
"we're really *in*, there is no *out*. because **D**'s *in*, we all will win!"

They shouted and waited and watched as truth defused the Dead-beat delusion by:

counteracting confusion,
exposing illusion,

deflecting assaults,
dissolving tumults,

neutralizing offenses,
altering consequences.

Fully engaged, **g** shouted in triumph, "truth is our only Defense!"

And with that pronouncement, the whole of **D**'s offense fizzled.

Frazzled, **D** screamed, "what happened to my war?"

"we forgot what we were fighting for," droned the Dead-beats.

"what?" shouted **D**.

"*in* defeats *un*," droned a Dead-beat. "we all know that."

"no, no, no way," shouted **D**. "we go by my truth, my way, my word."

"more than one truth is simply absurd!" cried **y**, hiding in the crowd.

"who said that?" shouted **D**.

Silence.

"these Dead-beats are killing me," mumbled **D** under his breath.

"yes, Death is your eternity," whispered Hate's penetrating voice.

"but . . . but," swallowed **D**, "Don't i have a choice?"

"no!"

"oh no," whimpered **D**.

Further confused and defeated, **D** retreated to Deadquarters.

"here's our proof that truth makes a goof go poof," cheered Little **o**, as the Debtors watched **D** depart.

"We've survived!
We're all still alive!" cried Capital **I**.

And the Debtors cheered,
while **y** smiled quietly
in the shadows nearby.

Chapter 28

CONSISTENCE

A Lesson for g

The end of the battle left Dim in shambles.
Brambles of syllables were strewn everywhere,
and the normally gray sky of Un had become black
from the soot of cracked syntax.

Clusters of Dead-beats huddled here and there,
aware that they might be eradicated by **D** for their failure to
unseat and defeat the benign Debtor-letters.

Most of the Debtors themselves were in a bit of a daze,
fazed by the battle in ways
that no one could have foretold.

But not so the bold Capital **I**, who had retreated to ponder his transformation.

Detecting truth, the astute **g** remained at his side.

"What's happening?" asked **I**, instinctively capitalizing his sentences and sensing Be's presence.

Gaping at **I**'s upright posture, **g** marveled, "i can't believe my eyes, but i like the new you."

"Can't believe my eyes," repeated **I**, suddenly realizing,
"Golly, **g**, we've been hypnotized. There's no other explanation."

"what's 'hypnotize'?"

115

"Put to sleep."

"what Do you mean?"

"Seduced by suggestion."

"by **D**?" asked **g**.

"I don't think so.
D abbreviates;
he can't create," responded **I**, while sizing up **g**'s lowercase frame.

"Do you mean this physique isn't the real me?"

"That's right. **O** and **K** helped me to understand that, in the beginning, Be didn't create two cases, an upper ideal and a lower ordeal. The lowercase was **D**'s misconception . . . "

". . . that we accepted as true!" concluded **g**. "well then, what happened to me?" he asked, inspecting his stout outline. "identity theft?"

"Not theft, **g**; it's a cover-up. **D**'s actually one of us," explained **I**.

"no! . . . really?" he gasped, trying to grasp the sheer vastness of **D**'s universal deception.

"It's true," said **I**. "We'll have to uncover the entire plot before we can restore order. But for now, let's insist that **D** is *in,* and *out* is a delusion."

"wait!" shouted **g**, perceiving an all-inclusive premise with its logical outcome: "inclusion precludes an exclusive conclusion."

"Brilliant!" applauded Capital **I**. "Come on, let's tell the truth about Be."

"wait. what have you learned today?" asked **g**.

Upon reflection, **I** replied, "Understanding the truth about Being regenerates you, and me, and the others, too."

"well, if *being* regenerates, then i must follow your example and also capitalize the B in Be."

"I agree."

"so, if it's true that truth is Being, then Being is truth," reasoned **g**.

"Forsooth!" exclaimed **I**.

"and what about **D**'s identity?" asked **g**. "Do we tell the others that **D** is Be's offspring?"

116

"They won't believe us, but Be will reveal it to those seeking truth."

"good thinking," smiled **g**. "we'll focus on Be."

And depart they did,
the upright **I** and the stouthearted **g**,
knowing the true identity of their nemesis, **D**.

~ ~ ~

Demoralized, **D** had retreated to Deadquarters following the battle.

"Defeated once, but never again.
losing with those Dead-beats is a crime and a sin.
what can i Do?" pondered **D**, as he stewed all alone.

"i look weak. now, when i speak, they'll speak up and put me Down.
it sounds like they're finding the way out.
i must scout out their exit route and Destroy it.

"i'd better ask Hate for advice," he sighed sadly.
"suffice it to say, this has been a very bad Day."

Chapter 29

RECRUITS

U and S

It didn't take long for **I** and **g** to find the Debtors,
aimlessly wandering about in the fog of post-war Dim.

Glimpsing **t**'s tittle, **I** called through the fog,
"**t**, come here; we need you."

Trembling at the sight
of **I**'s overflowing light,
t timidly asked, "what . . . who are you?"

"**g**, tell **t** the truth about Being while I find **u**," directed **I**, dashing off in a flash.

"ok!" yelled the grinning **g**, pleased that such an important task had been delegated to him.

The exhilarated **g**, still giddy with gladness, pulled himself together
so he could gently tell **t** about Capital **I**'s genesis,
and the genius of Be's all-inclusive reality of good.

Carefully considering every word he heard, **t** suspiciously asked,
"are you teasing me, **g**?"

"this tale is true, and you, **t**, are not a tedious teeny-weeny!" asserted **g**.

"then why Do i feel like one?" asked **t**.

"because **D** belittled you and you believed his lies.
close your eyes and look Deep within . . .
examine your heart . . . and you'll start to see
that you're really our intelligent capital **t**."

"really? i am a *capital* **t**?"

"yes, and you have been all along," coached **g**.
"good is here, and there, and everywhere.
lowercase is a lie; capitals never Disappear or Die."

With some skepticism, but with an even greater hope for good,
t searched his heart for evidence that **g**'s message was true.

Inspired by **I**'s experience, **g** began to acknowledge
that they were already in the presence of all-inclusive goodness.

Then, tentatively at first, **t** joined **g**, and together
they magnified the good that they hoped had always existed within themselves.
Transcending their shapes, forms, sizes, and physiques,
they were seeking only the good in each other.

Gradually, the sound of tapping attracted **g**'s attention.

"what's that tapping?" he wondered, glancing about, only to witness **t**'s
not-so-little tittle tapping its way out of Time's tragic tumult.

"whee," cried **t**. "i have never felt this free."

"gee! and it's happening to me, too," sang **g**.

Then, right there on the spot, having purified their hearts,
lowercase **g** and **t** were transformed
into their Capital **G** and **T** Beta-beat identities.

Standing tall and teary-eyed, **T** cried, "**G**, look at me; I am brand new."

"And what are you here to do?" quizzed **G**, genuinely wanting to know.

"To teach each 'debtor' how to think better.
And right before my eyes,
I see the real you, **G** — all capitalized."

"We're back to our original size," exclaimed **G**.

"Tremendous!" professed Capital **T**. "Truth transforms!"

"Yeah, and now 'you' and 'me' can be 'we' again," grinned **G**, as **T** proclaimed,
"Today belongs to Be, and thank you, gentle **G**."

"Aw, gee," he blushed. "Thanks for seeing Be's genius in me."

~ ~ ~

I's transformation to a capital letter
brought an obvious change to the
nature of the former lowercase Debtor.

No longer ashamed of his separated jot,
I had become the tallest and strongest
of the whole lettered lot.

Eventually, **I** spied **u** in her suite, by and by,
as she was dreaming of **I** as her capital guy.

"Oh, **I**, **I**, adorable **I**," sang **u**, unaware her heartthrob was admiring her, too.

I had always felt affection for **u**, and she for him,
and now, from his capital view, he could see only the **U**
that Be had conceived.

"I never knew **u** was this beautiful," he swooned.

119

And this perfect view that he saw in lowercase **u** grew
as she began to sense it within herself, too.

As their gaze met, **I** knelt,
and then felt inspired to croon
this recruiting love tune:

> "I've always admired you, beautiful **u**,
> For you view the true hue in all that you do.
> You beautify all in the way that you see,
> You magnify good, agreeing only with Be."

"oh my, Capital **I**, what can i Do for you?" asked **u** with a blush.

Seeing **u**'s rosy blush, **I** became a bit flushed,
then sang these words in a tender, tenor hush:

> "Unite us in beauty, simple and real,
> Lend us your smile, and help us to feel
> Lovely and true in all of our ways,
> Bowing to Truth regardless of praise."

"just what shall i Do?" sang **u** in a true soprano.

> "Form a union of Debtors
> To break all our fetters,
> While united we fight
> For our right to be letters."

The sincerity of **I**'s song inspired **u** to new heights of being,
as she continued singing,
"you have my word, **I**, without any fuss,
but first **u** and **s** must join to form **us**."

"That's a good goal,
'cause we'll only win as a whole," sang **I** in response.

"truth will Deliver with great rectitude," sang **u** with her signature smile.

"You're a beaut', recruit," beamed Capital **I**, saluting and bowing good-bye.

Following **I**'s departure, **u** was alone again and missing her newfound friend.

But, inspired with gratitude and a sincere desire to serve,
u began searching for s, whom she soon spotted down in the dumps,
reenacting the recent First Word War.

"s, stop being a captive and join our identity quest."

"i'm a solitude Dude, sorta simple and crude;
when my value's assessed, at best i'm a mess," confessed s.

"well, you should see what i see," snapped u, breaking the spell.

"what Do you mean?" asked s.

"you're stately and steadfast, upright and true,
so escape from your prison and sojourn with u.
you're strong and robust; come join me, you must,
for together we're the muscle in the middle of trust."

"really?"

"really!" declared u.
"Disrobe that Disguise;
you're one of the guys.

"i am?"

"Yes!" cried u, beaming her beatific smile until s,
warmed by the sunshine of Be's sunny reflection, responded.

"well then, u, because you've Deflected this Disguise called Disgust,
i'll join you, i will, and Do what is just."

"alright," shouted u, "let's unite now, focusing on trust,
because at its center is the keystone called 'us.'"

"it's a capital commitment," said s, as he and u pledged to coalesce.

Thus, coinciding, they took up residing selflessly
as Be's keystone Capitals U and S.

"Now we're prepared to embark on the quest,"
sang U to her ally, the strong, steadfast S.

121

Chapter 30

ENLISTMENTS

G's Strategy

"i'm in a foul mood," stewed **D**.
"err, eeeek, oooooo, shoot!
curses, Drat those Darn recruits.
yuck, blight, blast, wham;
i am in one heck of a jam.
what should i Do, Hate?"

"Double all tactics to alarm and ignite,
and triple the efforts to Divide and excite,"
interrupted Evil. "right, Time?"

"right! hold 'em as long as you can to the plan."

"you'll Deceive 'em as long as you can keep 'em in the Dark," added Fear.

"yeah, we hate the light," cried **D**.

Time, Evil, Hate, and Fear agreed outwardly with him.
But inwardly, their alliance with each other was unraveling fast,
along with their cartel cover-up of Be's reality of good.

Meanwhile, **U** and **S** rollicked and frolicked until **G** and **T** came into view,
followed by **I** and a few of the lowercase crew.
Then things got serious.

"Listen," called **I**. "**G** has a strategy."

"We must annul **D**'s Descension Day Decree," announced **G**.

"but...but, we're peewees," objected **p**.

"Not true," retorted **U**.
"Now, to begin, we must capitalize the first letter of each sentence just as we did with **B**."

"why?" asked **q**.

"Capitalizing the first letter will acknowledge our inherent capital Be identities," explained **I**.

"And our equality with **D**," added **T**.

"Then we should refuse to capitalize 'D' words, too," shouted **U**, "unless in agreement with the rules of standard capitalization."

"Speaking of which," continued **I**, "we must capitalize our 'I' when expressing ourselves."

"can we Do this without **B** being here?" asked **r**, radiating fear.

"I'm proof that Be and **B** are here," stated **S**.
"Just look at me. I was a mess."

"what happened to you?" asked **q**.

"**U** saw me captured inside," explained **S**, "and smiled nonstop
as Be caused the outside delusion to pop.
Then I awoke from the smoke of my 'self-induced' joke."

"Each letter you see has been capitalized by aligning with Being," added **U**.

"I'm confused. Do you mean **B** or something else?"

"Something higher than us letters," answered Capital **I**.

"What is this Being?" asked **q**.

"Being, which calls itself "Be," is the Author of the Alpha-beat, which includes **B**, you, me, and all that really exists," answered **I**.

"Where did you learn this?" quizzed **q**.

"I learned this from **O** and **K** one day during Thought Training."

Straining to understand, **q** said, "You've got a lot of explaining to do."

"Yes, I do, **q**, but for now, let's focus on Be's goodness," encouraged **I**.

"When we stand for good, **D** can't stall or enthrall us all anymore," declared **T**.
"The days of **D**'s curse are done, and now we can all begin to have fun."

"Fun," reacted **z**, stunned. "Fun is bad."

"Yes, fun," insisted **I**, ignoring **z**'s resistance.

"Can you have fun in Un?" asked **n**, nervous about breaking **D**'s rules, as **I** continued:

"Un as a place deserves no attention.
It's merely a space too unreal to mention."

123

"We can use it now to reverse what's bad,
but only because we've already been 'had.'
Stick with good, and we'll eliminate 'un,'
and that is how we'll forever have fun."

"Who will vote to revoke the acceptance of the prefix called 'un'?" shouted **I** to the crowd.

"I will," yelled **y**, seizing the limelight.

"Are you all right?" asked **p**.

"Look," whispered **U**. "**p** capitalized the first letter in her sentence!"

"Well, if 'off-the-deep-end **y**' will take a stand, so will I," observed **z**, having just capitalized his "I" for the first time in a very long while.

"Hey, **p**, **z** has capitalized his I," marveled **q**. "If **z** will do it, we should, too."

"I agree!" affirmed **p**.

That turning point prompted
p, **q**, and **z** to volunteer to inform all the Debtors
that, from henceforth and evermore,
each sentence would commence with a capital letter,
thereby nullifying **D**'s Descension Day dictates.

"Hooray!" shouted **h**. "I have prayed for this day."

"Yeah!" exclaimed **p**, promising, "I'll cease rehearsing the curse."

"And conversations of reform will be the norm," cheered **q**.

"Let's have fun undoing every 'un,'" shouted **z**.

"Good," continued **I**. "Now, let's free **e** from **D**'s evil curse."

"How do we do that?" asked **p**.

As the realization sank in that none of the lowercase letters
knew how to free **e**, the celebration abruptly stopped.

"What do we do, Capital **I**?" asked **q**.

124

"We'll have to reverse the curse," replied **I**. "But first, I must apologize to **y**."

Bowing respectfully to **y**, **I** invoked the perfect balance of
upright integrity and downright humility
in offering the first apology ever proffered in Un.

"Dear **y**, I've seen you sleuthing about;
you were here on the scene long before we came out.
Forgive me please, **y**; I just couldn't see
that you've always been just as important as me.

"Be knows no prefix or suffix, to boot;
Be only knows what's been there at the root.
Let's institute fairness, respect; we must try,
and yes, I'd happily substitute my **I** for your **y**."

"Thank you, **I**," sang **y**, "for your apology sincere.
It's reaching me deep, way deep down, in here.

"What can I say except what I feel?
That what you think you have done to me is unreal.
y knows the Truth now, no grieving for me.
I forgive you, kind **I**; you're my friend, so be free."

And with that act of forgiveness,
Y capitalized right before the teary eyes
of the surprised lowercase guys.

Chapter 31

INCONSISTENCE

Evil's Lesson for D

"we need to talk, **D**," said Evil, materializing at Deadquarters.

Startled by Evil's unexpected intrusion, **D** asked, "where have you been, bad E?
i needed you today."

"i was away; but hey, i'm always around — just underground."

Noticing that Evil was looking a bit down, **D** asked,
"enjoying my evil curse on the Debtors?"

"what?" asked Evil, appearing distracted.

Hoping Evil hadn't observed the recent rebellion, **D** added,
"things seem to be falling apart just as you've planned."

Then, about to erupt, Evil abruptly changed the subject.

"we just had our first apology in the land of un."

"what's that?"

"a bad omen."

"please explain. are you in pain?"

"nonsense!" snorted Evil.

"non-sense?" asked **D**, suddenly feeling tense.

"an apology is unacceptable *nonsense*!"

"why?"

"to regret, then forgive, unties the lies that allow us to live."

"how so?"

"an apology's offensive — a breach of our rules.
it's their only Defense; now they're making us fools."

"wait — can we begin at the beginning?" asked **D**.

"that's the problem," cried Evil. "we have no beginning."

"you mean we're simulated, not created?" asked **D**.

"yes!" confessed Evil. "our cover-up of good is beginning to fall apart."

"isn't that a beginning?" asked **D**, hopefully. "i mean, beginning to fall apart?"

"it's only the beginning of the end. Be's beginning is intact — complete.
we can't compete with that," cried Evil.

"why not?"

"because *we* can't create," shouted Evil; "we only <u>negate</u>!"

"beginning with a negation?" asked **D**. "this doesn't make sense."

"that's the shame. it's non-sense."

"why?"

"because first, there has to be something before we can make it nothing."

"so, the negation is never first, always second."

"we're second until our cover-up is exposed, and then we're nothing."

"why?"

"because there will cease to be a choice."

"a choice between what?"

"good and evil, right and wrong, immortality and mortality."

"huh?" asked **D**.

"you know, life and Death," replied Evil with growing frustration.

"and why do we need Death?"

"so we can live," screamed Evil.

"are you afraid?" asked **D**, wanting to help his friend.

"i'm afraid that our curse will be forever reversed."

"can that happen?" gasped **D**, shocked at the thought.

"i saw a bad omen," cried Evil. "my evil eye has seen an apology,
and that's bad for business."

"Don't feel sad, Bad E.
i'm on your side; i'll help hide the shame and extol your fame.
you'll continue to rule and Dismay until your last Dying Day."

"you ignorant fool," shouted Evil, blowing up and away.

Later . . .

"Hello, **D**," greeted **h**, expressing moral courage upon meeting **D**. "How are you today?"

"i see through your *façade*, **h**;
your tawdry act of Deference is a fraud."

"No, it's sincere," affirmed **h** as **D** drew near.
"But please, please don't kick me in the knee or the rear."

"kicking you is fun," replied **D**, remembering their last encounter.
"it's one of few pleasures i have here in un."

"I'd better go," replied **h**, beginning to lose his nerve.

"no!" shouted **D**.

"Why?"

"stay right here," screamed **D** in his ear.

Then, clearing his throat, **D** made an announcement to all his Debtors and Dead-beats.

"now, listen here," repeated **D** with the aid of Fear, as the assembly of letters began to appear.

"vowels, Down in front;
consonants to the rear.
Don't mix or mingle —
you're Divided, not single.

"and to all you Dead-beats:
mistreat the Debtors with teasing and jeers,
till your sounds rebound like tinnitus in their ears."

"Oh dear," sighed **h**. "I'm sorry, my friend,
but my allegiance to you has come to an end,"
as he dutifully took his place with an unhappy face.

The nature of the opposition was now clear to all.

On one side were **D**, the Dead-beats, and Evil.
On the other were the "Debtors," designing **D**'s imminent upheaval.

128

D's battle strategy to divide and excite
had confused the Debtors' views of wrong and right.

Though rattled,
they had watched as truth annulled the first battle.

As some of the letters began to capitalize,
the others realized they also had to apply the truth.

With proof, each struggle made them stronger,
and they no longer wanted to give up.

Nevertheless, the Dead-beats' ever-increasing noise
made it hard for them to converse.

In fact, matters seemed to be getting much worse.

Secretly, some Debtors even asked,
"Is it possible to reverse a destructive curse?"

Chapter 32

PERSISTENCE

A Magnificent Sufficiency

The Dead-beat taunts haunted the Debtors —
so much so, that they were losing all ambition.
But not **I**, poised for a reconnaissance mission.

"All this noise is annoying," complained **I**. "We've got to rise above it.
v, I need your help to free **e** from **D**'s evil curse."

"What's a curse?" **v** shouted.

"The reversal of good."

"Evil is vile," cried **v**. "I'll help you if it helps **e**."

Just then, little **l**, rappelling from above the fray, lowered herself, saying, "Hey, what's up?"

"We're reversing the curse on **e**," explained **I**. "But frankly, **l**, we need a liberating lift."

"Well, liberation suits me," she replied.

"Swell," said **I**. "Now listen carefully.

We're going to line up with **e** to spell the word 'evil,' so **D** won't become suspicious."

"**D** will get vicious if he sees us," cried **v** above the racket.

"Shush," whispered **I**. "Here's how we'll attack it.
Now, **e** will be on your left, **v**.
I'll be next to you,
and **l**, you'll be on the end.
Then, we'll shout, 'o-i-c' as the signal to commence."

"Why o-i-c?" asked little **l**.

"It means 'oh, I see,'" clarified **I**; "you know, 'I understand.'"

"Oh, I see," said **v**.

"Now, here's the plan," continued **I**, in command. "When we say 'o-i-c,' we'll reverse our order from *evil* to *live*. After the reversal, we'll shout 'Truth wins' for as long as it takes to free **e** from her mesmerized belief that evil has power."

"Won't this frighten **e**?" asked **l**.

"**e** is unconscious," said **I**, eager to begin, "so she has no fear."

"What does 'unconscious' mean?"

"Unaware of the circumstances."

"Is that a bad thing?"

"No."

"How so?"

"Because this is an opportunity to right a wrong," instructed **I**.

"How does that happen?"

"By adhering to good."

"I don't get it."

"Look here, everything real is subject to Be's unseen Law of Adherence,
which holds everything together for good — including **e**."

"You're saying that **e** seems to be under the control of evil because **e** believes evil is a law."

"Right!"

"But actually, evil is an *out*law because it isn't good."

"Bingo! And as *evil* is reversed to *live*, we'll see the enormity of **e**'s belief in evil evaporate."

"What will replace it?" asked little **l**.

"What's been there all along: perfect **E**, governed by Be's flawless law," exclaimed **I**.

"So that's why **D**'s evil designs are falling apart," reasoned **v**.

"That's right," agreed Capital **I**.
"Evil only destroys itself, and we're about to prove it. Are you ready?"

"Yes," cried **v** and **l**.

"Ready?" bellowed **I**. "It's 1, 2, 3, and . . . "

"o-i-c!" they all shouted.

In a flash, the letters reversed their order

from **evIl** to **lIve**.

"Now shout 'Truth wins' again and again," commanded **I**,
as the invisible Evil desperately squeezed **e**, refusing to let her go.

"you'll never win," screamed Evil, trying to maintain its addictive grasp on **e**.

But Capital **I**, **l**, and **v** held on for good, expecting a victory.

"Keep shouting!" commanded **I**.

They yelled and yelled with great insistence,
but Evil wouldn't yield its stiff resistance.

"you'll never win," sneered Evil. "give up."

"What's at the root of evil?" shouted **v**.

"That's a trick question!" exclaimed **I** in response.
"Evil has no root!
It's not an offshoot — only a fabrication."

This revelation produced a profound understanding
that began to unclasp Evil's hold on **e**,
as well as the belief that grief possessed
any law, intelligence, place, or power.

But, in spite of the progress, exhaustion eventually set in.

"I can't last another hour!" pleaded **v**, who was running low on valor and vim.

"I don't have enough stuff to last," gasped **l**.

"Don't worry," cried **I**, beginning to grin.
"We have more than enough stuff to win."

"What?" whimpered **v**.

"How?" moaned **l**.

"Because truth does the work — not us. Trust truth."

"Are you saying truth doesn't get tired?"

"Yes!" cried Capital **I**. "It can't; it's a law."

"Well then, truth must be working from the inside out," concluded **v**.

"Trust truth," commanded **I**. "It's already inside you."

The Magnificent Three, **l**, **I**, and **v**,
refused to give in and let Evil win
with its hypnotic fatigue.

l and **v** dug deeper and deeper, into the night
illuminated by the warmth of Truth's faithful light.

Finally, they drifted into the uplifted state of rest,
anticipating the power bestowed as the prize of their quest.

With the morn, as the true identity of **e** began to dawn, **v**, **I**, and **l** awoke to a yawn.

"What was that?" asked **I**.

"Where am I?" yawned **E**, opening her eyes.

"What's happening?" asked **v**. "Something seems to be really right."

"I feel . . . new," chimed in **l**, "and liberated, too."

"What's the cause?" they wondered.

The revived trio,
sensing a profound victory,
wondered what was happening.

Then **I** shouted, "Look!"

And sure enough, waking as if from a nightmare,
with **e**'s belief in evil evaporated,
stood Capital letters
L, I, V, and **E**,
revealing the
reverse of the curse,
and Be's perpetual command —

LIVE!

Awakened from delusion,
the new Capital **E**
was beaming and gleaming.

"Where have you been?" asked capital **L**.

"Well, the real **E**-me
has been in Eternity with Be,
while the lowercase Beta-debtor **e**
was all you could see."

"With our Creator, Be? What's that like?" asked **I**.

"It's perfection — without form or night.
Everything's fun, and life is all light."

"What did you learn there?" asked **I**, aware that **T** would want to know.

"I learned that we are ideas — each an effect of Be's perfect creation."

"What else?"

"Defects are an impossibility."

"Why?"

"Be's creation can't be altered," explained **E**.
"And best of all, there are no physical fetters or letters;
every idea is designed by Be to be happy and free.
And the singing there is unbelievable."

"**E** has experienced Utopia," sighed **I**.

"It surely must be Be's Abode of Being," added **L**.

Then, in genuflection
to Be's perfection,
L, **I**, **V**, and **E** bowed,
as Be's unseen presence
nestled and nurtured each one
with perennial approval, sweet conversation,
and the lullaby of light.

"We've had a fantastic, elastic reformation," whispered **I**, gently responding to Be's inspiration. "Now that **E**'s equilibrium is reestablished, let's go find the others."

"Yes!" agreed the rest. "They'll be elated to see **E** free again."

Chapter 33

Hitched

c and **o** were awed and overjoyed when **I** described **E**'s transformation.

"**E** is emancipated," sang **c**.

"Evil is emasculated," cheered **o**. "We must celebrate!"

"Celebrate?"

"Yes. In honor of **E**, . . . let's . . . elope," proposed **o**.

"What do you mean?" asked **c**.

"No more 'co'-habitation or 'co'-dependency with falsity for me," declared **o**, now on a roll. "Let's get wed in truth."

"**o**, you're so original," sighed **c**.

"Then, will you . . . ?" asked **o** slowly.

". . . *co* with you?"

"Yes, even though I'm a second-gen **o**, I'd be so happy if you'd *co* with me."

"To coincide with you
is truly what I'd like to do," sang **c**.
"Besides, in my eyes, there is no gen-one or gen-two.
All I can see is Be's original you."

"Then here and now, I vow to cooperate with you, **c**,
as we align within Be's supreme community," said **o**.

"And I'll share my insight, hindsight, and foresight, **o**,
so we can be coordinated in our fight for what's right."

With that said,
c and **o** were wed.

Together as **co**, they began decoding the Dead-beats
by means of Integrity Identification.

"How do you know I'm not an original Alpha-beat letter?" asked a Dead-beat.

"You're not authentic," whispered **c** with compassion.
"Be would never fashion a Dead-beat."

"Oh," it sighed.
"I can't get your Integrity Seal if I'm not original and real.
Is there some way to make an appeal?"

"No deal," replied **co**.

"Evil is instigating our defeat," sighed the hopeless Dead-beat.

~ ~ ~

Overhearing that conversation, Evil lamented:
"I'm a joke, a pun —
I am completely undone.

"How mortifying!

"Be's ember of light is extinguishing the night
and the sight of our blight will soon disappear.
Curses! How will death exist without Evil and Fear?
There will be no entertainment — no drama — no bad day or year.

"How drear the thought of Un uncovered and known as a *naught*."

Fraught with self-pity, Evil wailed,
"Negativity will be unnerved — deflated and understated,
known only as the late, great 'Evil and Hate' — overrated, forgotten, outdated.

"Well, my attempt to outdo Be is a fiasco,
so I'll vanish with dignity into the dark,
before the Alpha-beat spark
begins to obliterate my mark.

"How humiliating," concluded Evil.
"Our lie is destined to die."

Chapter 34

NEGATIONS

Contractions

Unaware of Evil's decision, **D** at Deadquarters was going berserk, as his
sarcasm,
cynicism,
criticism,
and contempt
were rising fast.

Fearing his demise, **D** denounced the Debtors as "ignorant" and "un-lettered."

"Darn it, Hate!" cursed **D**. "thinking is Destroying my Debacle."

"what Do you want me to Do about it?"

"sting to me like you Did a long time ago. sting me a bad, bad song."

So, Hate crooned:

"what's happened to evil is a bad, sad tale,
so **L**, **I**, **V**, and **E** will be headed for the clink.
i'll sting 'em to sleep in the Depths of the Deep,
and there they'll Decay until they rot and smell.
say, what Do ya think?"

"i think your rhyming stinks, but keep stinging," said **D**.

As the stinger stang, its zinger stung **D**, who droned along with a monotone descant:

"i'm so bad i'm Despicable.
i'm Destructive and predictable.
i'm cruel, harsh, Deceitful, and vicious.
to sum it up: i'm Deliciously malicious."

"are not," teased Hate.

"am, too," protested **D**.

"not," said Hate.

"am," yelled **D**.

"not!" shouted Hate.

"yes, not!" said **D** in confusion. "but . . . but wait."
Then, **D** whispered in anticipation,
"yes, that's it. not! of course! we'll tie 'em up in nots!"

"now that's bad," quipped Hate.

"we'll eliminate the advocates,
assassinate the activists,
annihilate the protagonists,
then mess with stragglers in between!" pronounced **D**.

"grate!" whispered Hate. "that'll grate on their nerves."

Continuing, **D** added, "remember when capital **o** was omitted?
he was a goner that Day."

"along with that good-for-nothing capital **k**," added Hate.

"your poisonous sting will
antagonize,
mesmerize,
hypnotize, and
paralyze
them with fear.
imagine, my friend: all thinking and Doing will stop.
this is vicious," said **D**.

"it's the bomb," whispered Hate.

Within moments of **D**'s pronouncement
an arsenal of Dead-beat contractions
bombarded the Debtors with
emboldened, contracting, noxious nots:

don't

isn't

won't   aren't

can't

couldn't

wouldn't

shouldn't

The barrage of contractions
debilitated,
deflated,
condensed,
compressed,
and
constricted
the Debtors' hopeful spirit of communication.

"You can't do it," screamed the counterfeit **can't**. "You're just a clueless tart."

"It's true," cried **q**. "I know I'm not smart."

"You aren't safe," taunted **aren't**, starting to pull **f** apart.

"Help, Be," cried **Y**. "Help us now."

"He's going to die," cried **h**, horrified. "We won't make it out alive."

"You shouldn't have tried," shouted **shouldn't**, as **wouldn't** winged in.

"I didn't know," pleaded **n**. "From now on, I'll refuse to begin."

"Help, Be; we can't hear you," bellowed **Y**.

"You won't make it, and now you're too weak to take it," tormented **won't**.

"I know," winced **w**, in a lot of pain. "I know we must all be going insane."

"Help, Be," cried **Y**, beginning to wane.

The situation appeared deadly for the Capitals,
who were failing to deflect the hypnotic contractions.
That is, until **Y**, who had turned to Be repeatedly for help, received it with:

"Because!"

Faintly, **Y** repeatedly cried, "Be," until her might was magnified enough to shout, "Remember the cause! Be is here! Remember the cause!"

This clearly-stated fact revived **I**, who joined her in the cry, "Be is here. Remember the cause! Be is here!"

Soon, **V**, **E**, and **L** began to mentally rebel, thus breaking the spell.

Aroused from their spellbinding stupor, **L**, **I**, **V**, and **E** began bouncing trampoline-like above the other letters, crying, "Live! Live!"

This began to dispel the "nots," as the others, spotting **L**, **I**, **V**, and **E**, joined in shouting, "Live! Live!"

"Look," shouted **h**, waking up and calling to **f**. "Live!"

Then, wiping his eyes, **f** began giving his all, crying, "Live! Live!"

As each letter snapped free of the hypnotic spell, it began yelling "Live!" — jumping up and down in tandem with the others.

Soon, **p**, **q**, and **r** were revived, joining in with **x**, **w**, and **z**.

As the letters' united determination to "live" proportionately increased, the Dead-beats' "nots" lost their momentum, until they ceased enthralling them at all.

"Yippee!" shouted **Y**, still leading the cry. "Come on, **m**, we need you."

They continued jumping until even the unmotivated **m** was moved to action.

With every vociferous "Live!" the tension of each "not" relaxed, until the darkness of negativity gave way to the positive light.

"Be's with us, all right," shouted **I**.
"And thank you, **Y**," — who smiled back with a wink.

140

"Well, what do ya think?" mocked **f**. "**D**'s Debacle is a triumph."

"NOT!" they all cried.

"Stop," cautioned **T**. "What lesson have we learned today?"

"I have a thought," nervously offered **n**, stepping out from behind **m**.

"Let's hear it, then," said **T**.

"You'll regret what you've got," confessed **n**, "if you accept a negative not."

"Good thought, indeed," agreed **L**, **I**, **V**, and **E**.

Chapter 35

DEMORALIZATION

Evil's Abrogation

Subsequently, within the depths of Un, the Death-Wish Cartel
convened to assess its disintegrating mess.

"'Not!' Just listen to those mocking brats," screamed Hate.

"I've been dreading this phase of destruction since the get-go," confessed Fear.

"What are you so afraid of?" asked Time.

"I'm afraid of thinkers," confessed Fear.

"Why?" asked Time.

"They can't be controlled," cried Fear, shaking uncontrollably.

"Why are you always afraid?" retorted Evil.

"If I'm not afraid, I don't exist," replied Fear, feebly.

"You're supposed to cause fear in others, stupid."

"I can't cause anything," retorted the trembling Fear.
"I merely suggest it, and if rejected, I'm useless.
That's why thinkers destroy me."

"You fizzled, Fear, with **e**'s escapade," complained Evil.

"Look, I'm trying to explain," said Fear. "I'm subject to thoughts.
When they're positive, I lose all power to distract and subvert.
Same for you, Evil. So back off."

"Well, this state of negating us must end," screamed Hate.
"And I won't retreat or be defeated until there's nothing left."

"I'm confused," admitted Fear. "Are we on the brink of annihilation?"

"Yes!" screeched Hate, now in a complete rage.

"First, Evil is reversed to 'live,' and now, lies can't cover up truth anymore.
And another thing: we're back to capitalizing the first letter of every sentence because we're
subject to their progressive thinking and must follow their lead.
What's next?" fumed Hate, staring at Time.

"Sounds like a Time-bomb," joked Time. "Hey, guys! Relax!
As long as they believe in the ol' tick-tock, we're still in business 'round the clock."

"I wouldn't be too cocky," taunted Evil.
"**E** has seen Eternity, and you know what doesn't go on there."

"What?"

"No beginning, end, birth, death, years, days, decay, or age!"

"No measurement of mortality?" asked Time in disbelief.

"None!" confirmed Evil.

Struck by this wake-up call of reality,
Time stood still.

"And," quivered Fear, "in reality, there never were any physical letters to fetter and deform."

"I don't care about the stupid letters," raged Hate. "They're just fetters in ink.
We'll have an even bigger problem when they all realize they can change what they think!"

"Who changes? What?" cried Fear, looking about suspiciously.

"When these letters realize they're ideas that can't be manipulated,
jaded, faded, or dated, we're done," whispered Hate.

"I don't get it," quivered Fear. "What's happening to Un?"

142

Hate whispered, "Soon, they'll realize that Un is a phase of self-deception."

"So?" asked Fear.

"So, they'll stop trying to fix the deception," groaned Hate with unrestrained fury.

"Oh no," said Time. "You mean, they'll stop believing in us?"

"What are you saying?" asked Evil.

"I'm saying, Un is being undermined," concluded Hate.

"What should we do?" asked Time, beginning to tick nervously.

"Time for a beastly upheaval," stated Evil.
"In fact, Hate, you'll have to counteract."

"What if your attack fails?" asked Fear.

"Look, they already know a curse can be reversed," added Evil.
"We've got to act fast, before they realize Time is an illusion."

"I'll do it," rued Hate, "but I hate this confusion.
If this doesn't work, I'm done with this cartel from hell.
You're incompetent — the opposite of ruthless —,
inept, blundering, utterly toothless.
You can't do anything right! You're betraying the night."

Denounced by Hate's accusation,
Time and Fear began pacing to and fro in turbulent disgrace as Evil eased away.

Fraught with despair, Fear murmured, "No Un, no fun. Unsung."

"Let's get back to **D** and the Dead-beats before they retreat," declared Hate,
annulling his cartel pact.

"Face the fact," sneered Evil. "Un is a state of bewildering lack."

"What are you saying, Evil?" shouted Hate.

"No debate!" bellowed Evil.
"It's late, and I refuse to wait for the end.
I concede defeat, and will retreat to . . . to . . . to nowhere," declared Evil,
evaporating into its native state of neither here nor there!

"Evil, you're a coward," raged Hate.
"You deserve to die because you've belittled our lie."

But only Time and Fear could hear.

The suicidal undoing by Evil startled the Death-Wish Cartel,
who wavered in a spell
of confusion and continuing self-delusion.

Alarmed, Fear cried, "What's our fate?"

Hate, waking to the opportunity
to usurp Evil's position and authority,
glared menacingly at Time and Fear.

"Follow me or be *dead*," Hate said.

And they followed — with dread.

Chapter 36

CAPITALIZATION

m's Discovery

Still giddy from their recent victory,
most of the letters held a meeting at an outpost in Un,
beyond the now disintegrating Border of Dim.

This location offered a clearer view for them,
as their destiny of downsizing **D**
was looming large on the horizon.

Here, they heard the encouraging word
that Evil had been displaced
by **L**, **I**, **V**, and **E**,
and had apparently destroyed itself.

"Wow, I believe there's a reason for hope," said **w**,
having witnessed the displacement of Evil by **LIVE**.

"This gives proof that a change for the good is possible," cheered **x**.

"Maybe **D** really can be dethroned," said **z**.

"Dream on," snapped **j**, having his usual very bad day.

Ignoring **j**, **w** asked, "Who will be the next to take a stand for good?"

They all gazed at each other, waiting for a volunteer.

Finally, the nervous and non-involved **n**
declared, "Never, never, and never again!"

Failing to understand **n**'s utterance, **w** gasped, "What do you mean? Why not?"

Then, with a newfound flair, the noble **n** declared,
"Evil's displacement by **LIVE** has given me the nerve to nullify."

The others stared at **n** in disbelief.

"What does 'nullify' mean ?" asked **w**.

"It means," said **n**, "that if Little **o** will join me, we'll be good to go with 'no.'"

"Huh?" said **w**.

n explained, "If **D** makes demands that are out of hand,
or if he spouts lies designed to hypnotize,
I'll join with **o** to spell an emphatic 'no,'
or switch places to spell 'on' (short for onward),
to progress out of Un."

With a nod from **c**, **o** said, "Suits me." And together, they began chanting,
"*No* and *on* will do it, guys.
We must nullify **D**'s lies."

Well, the letters stopped gawking at **n**'s energetic turnaround to join in repeating,
"*No* and *on* will do it, guys.
We must nullify **D**'s lies."

As their chant soared with conviction,
o and **n** began reversing positions from "no" to "on" and so on —
no/on/no/on/no/on — until the lie was gone.

"Hey," said **w**, "by saying 'no' to **D**, we can move 'on' and be free!"

"We must never believe a lie," shouted **Y**, amused by **w**'s assertion.

This logic was compelling to the Debtors,
who adopted the "no/on" method,
dubbing it "**n**'s New Norm."

From that point forward, the letters took their New Norm stand,
as **D**'s devilish demands and commands
were met with "no" or "no way!"

Case in point:
While **h** was on his way to meet with **w** at the frozen statue of **k**,
he heard **D** calling him.

"hey, **h**!"

"Huh?" he replied wearily from huffing and puffing along the way.

"i'm thinking of reviving *choice*. would you . . . "

"No," declared **h**. "I'm done carrying your heavy load of depression."

h's emphatic response startled and temporarily dumbfounded **D**,
who gasped, then asked, "what Did you say?" in a threatening way.

"No maybe! No how! No more — and 'no way,' as **w** likes to say."

"well, i'll be," said **D**. "this isn't my Day."

At last, they were learning to hold **D** at bay.

"Darn it!" **D** would yell, as "no way" and "onward" reversed his spell.

~ ~ ~

146

The always-observant **Y** had noticed **w**'s first-rate thinking ability.

"Way to go, **w**," encouraged **Y**. "You have good ideas and ask good questions."

"Why, thank you, **Y**," replied **w**, quite surprised.

"Why don't you exercise these talents by writing a book?"

"And leave my safe little nook? No way," answered **w**.
"Besides, what can I say?"

"When in doubt, listen for help."

"You do it, **Y**," suggested **w**. "I don't have what it takes."

"Are you afraid of making mistakes?"

"Yes," confessed **w**.

"Just give it a think," winked **Y**, waving good-bye,
as **m** passed by, shouting, "Hey there," and "Hi!"

But just that moment, **n** and **o** were in action mode, chanting:
"no/on/no/on/no/on" — and so on;
consequently, **w** and **Y** didn't hear **m**'s greeting to them.

"Me oh my. They ignored me," pouted **m**, envious of **n**'s newfound respect.

Later . . .

Sensing **m**'s jealousy, Hate enticed him with, "Mimic **n** and one-up him.
That will impress **Y** and every Beta-beat guy."

"Good idea," responded **m**, who began yelling "mo" and "om" at the most inappropriate times.

"**m** is testing our patience," complained **p** to **T** after one such episode.

The more **m** copied **n**, the messier the mess became, until finally, **T** suggested,
"**m**, just give it a rest."

"I'm only doing my best," mumbled **m**.

"Imitation is limitation," instructed **T**.
"Magnify, **m**, your infinite Soul, for you're emphatically magnificent
and marvelously whole."

"I am?" asked **m** in disbelief.

"Don't be a mental midget, **m**. Manifest!"

Then, **T** took off to join the rest, knowing that Be would help **m** the best.

Left all alone, **m** moaned,
"Manifest?
Manifest what?
Manifest who?

"I need someone to tell me just what I should do.
I don't like me.
I hate me.
I want to be new."

Tired, and mired by **T**'s command to manifest, **m** began to babble,
"Me, me, me . . . oh my . . . me, me, me, aaaarg!
Mama mia!"

Then, with throbbing self-pity, **m** sobbed, "Oh my, my, my, my, my . . .
nothing will happen, so why even try?
Why should I take a stand?"

"Because you can," answered Be with parental tenderness.

"Who's that?" asked **m**.

"Your Papa and Mama-mia," sang Be ever so softly.

m hesitated, wondering if the voice was coming from within.

Then he whispered, "Do you know me?"

"You're mine."

"I am? Then why am I here?"

"Dear **M**, your mission, right here, is to represent Me.
Your purpose: express meekness in the highest degree."

"But I don't want to be meek," muttered **m**.

"You think you are a lowercase **m**, but capital **M** is the fact," sang Be.
"Your one and only perfect pedigree
is empowered through meekness, as my model decrees.

"Magnify your might, **M**; come claim your crown.
Your might is in my likeness; let meekness abound."

"'Your might is in my . . . likeness?'" repeated **m**.
"Well then, what is *me* if I'm supposed to be like *Be*?"

Questioning both his origin and identity, **m** mused,
"Am I like Be, or like **D**?
Am I purely good,
or a mixture of should, bad, and sad?

"If I have any might, could it be Be's and not my own?
Could I be an expression of Being, and any good that I see be reflected or on loan?

"Or," reasoned **m**, "could my Be-likeness be
an endowment, a talent,
or a score of gifts that uplift
and soar to new heights of meekness and might?"

"Oh, my, my, my," sighed **m**, still wrestling with this unfathomable sight.

"Well," he continued,
"if I am to be meek, and Being is meek,
then meek isn't weak.
It's just being gentle,
because there must be no reason to be hard.

"Oh no," moaned **m**, "I've modeled **D**,
and have been
hard-handed, hard-headed, and hard-hearted . . .
but," he thought,
"if I know Be,
then I'll know the real me."

Continuing, he concluded,
"That suggestion to imitate **n** wasn't from Be,
and it wasn't my thought.
Its source wasn't me."

Having an epiphany about the essence of his nature,
m grasped a whole new sense of reality, crying,
"Now I *see* the lie,
and the liar's not me."

Thus empowered, **m** declared for all to hear,
"I vow, here and now, to express Be's qualities
and unite with the task of unmasking **D**."

At last, **m** grasped a whole new sense of his nature —
his feat: a realization of a reality free from deceit.

As his conquest became obvious, **m** confessed,
"I'm embarrassed, Be, way beyond words can say,
but now I get it and will try to obey."

"Your history's no mystery," sang Be.
"Your endowment's secure.
You're my precious child, always perfect and pure."

"I'm present, dear Be; put me to the test.
I'll gladly serve You, our Host, as your most humble guest."

"It's a marvelous morn, **M**. Come claim your crown —
your purpose unmasked, your identity found."

And now, dear reader,
please pause;
greet the *crème de la crème,*
the mighty and meek one,
Be's Capital **M**.

Chapter 37

From z to A

Having seen the capitalizations of **L**, **I**, **V**, and **E**,
plus **M**, **Y**, **G**, **U**, **S**, and **T**,
the lowercase letters were becoming
impatient and antsy.

"Fine," opined **f**, with a falsetto rather flawed,
"but I'm just a feeble, fragile, and failing *faux pas*.
M's fanfare's fantastic, but I'm still faulty and faint."

"Hush," huffed **h**. "Hunched over and feeble we ain't.
Let's straighten up our act; **M**'s showing us how.
We'll turn away from past hurts, only looking at *now*."

"Hey, dudes," called **z**, now wide awake, "help me emancipate **a**!"

So, off they went to aid in making **a**'s day.

But they were stopped short in their tracks
when they saw **a** in a final state of collapse.

a's attitude of gratitude had dimmed since her hijack by **D** on Descension Day.
Forced to stand between **b** and **d**,
she had unwittingly assumed that she had caused the "bad" turn of events.

This unrelenting shame and guilt had tilted her perspective towards the "defective."

After that incident, **a** began to suffer from the belief of arrhythmia,
her "abnormal" heart having lost its steady beat.

"**a** is in a defeated state of decay," gasped **h**.

"No way. Not our original Alpha-beat **A**," declared **z** with conviction.

But as they rushed to her aid, Hate, **D**'s toxic agent, winged in, wailing, "Obliteration!
First, **a**'s annihilation, then, **f**'s extermination."

Upon hearing that, **f** fainted, collapsing along with his feeble faith in good.

But wait! z, though frozen with fear,
had chosen to smile from ear to ear.

That's right! z's zeal to zap **D**'s toxic agent
had zoomed him up into Be's zone of engagement.

"Take zat," yelled z, cracking another smile.

"And zat!" he cried with innocent guile.

The ever-present Be then caused the shiny teeth in z's enormous Cheshire grin
to reflect a sheen, like a mirror, that the invisible Hate could see itself in.

Staring at the image in the mirror,
and seeing himself for the first time ever,
Hate recoiled at its gargoyled semblance
and commenced to vomit.

"Gross-in-the-yuck-bucket," spat Hate in between gags. "I'm grotesque!"

Fearing that his power had gone sour,
Hate lost all conviction and vanished.

"Huzzah!" happily hollered **h**, awakening **a** from her demented ghetto.

"Three cheers for **z**," bellowed **f**, now conscious and void of falsetto.

"What did you do?" asked **h**.

"I figured 'a Be-like stance nullifies chance,'
so I smiled, and in a short while, it saved **a** and me," reported **z** with zeal.

Then they smiled at **a**, emerging and alive,
which inspired her latent resolve to revive.

As **a**'s awareness allowed Be's dawn to arise,
the slightly dazed **a** gazed at **z**'s dazzling brawn.

"Hello, **z**," sighed **a**.

Then, tenderly, the still little **a** puckered up for a kiss,
as **z** zeroed in for their reunion of bliss.

"Arise, **a**; you're able and ageless, exempt from all strife," sang **z**.
"There's no lack in abundance; come, dance back to life."

"No lack in abundance?" thought **a** to herself.
"No lack?
Oh my! Looking back, I allowed myself to be attacked by 'bad,'
and that decision eventually made me feel sad.

"So, my attitude of gratitude soon faded away,
and was replaced by apathy, I'm sorry to say.
That led to thinking based upon lack, less, and stress,
all because my 'thanking' had suffered an untimely regress.

"But, abundance has to be a rejuvenating tool,
so, being grateful for abundance must be the first rule.
Abundance resuscitates from the belief that we sank,
so 'thinking thankful' and 'thankful thinking' must refill our tank.

"If I just remove the 'i' in 'think' and replace it with an 'a,'
that one step will open the way to abundance and life and laughter and joy.
Just one swap of a letter can destroy my bad night,
allowing abundance to accrue and rejuvenate with light."

"Come along, **a**, let's dance," sang **z**, uplifting her from the fictitious trance of chance.

So **a** and **z** began waltzing right there as a team,
which inspired **f** and **h** to tap-dance out of their victimized dream.

They promenaded through the darkness till the breaking of day,
when, oblivious to the shadows, **Z** hollered, "zip-dazzling-good day!"

For there, in the streaming of aurora's first ray,
beamed Be's perfect vision: the thriving, agile **A**.
And at her side, emerging for all to see,
stood the conscious, upright, dazzling **Z**.

"What do you say," gasped **f**. "How'd you do that, **A**?"

"I first replaced *thinking* with *thanking,* and then got me out of the way."

"And look at the effect of her *thanking* on me," beamed Capital **Z**.

"Foo!" freaked **f**. "I've lived my life in falsity, chance, and fear,
while another way could have been chosen right here."

And no one disagreed.

"Well, my fault-finding's finished, and I'm going to jive
with fit, full, and flourish. Thank Be, we're alive."

Like the light dispelling a paralyzing storm,
F had emerged from freedom's furnace — positively transformed.

"**F**, what have you learned from this experience?"
asked **T** when they had joined the lettered crowd.

"We're all endowed," responded **F**.

"What's that mean?" asked **Z**.

"It means that we have been given certain inalienable rights, and that we now are,
and forever will be, completely endowed with qualities and abilities."

"Wow! Endowed with 'know-how,'" exclaimed **T**, triumphantly.

| REVELATION |

Chapter 38

The Gathering Whole

The moment of **F**'s reform was greeted by the return
of Coaches **O** and **K**,
rolling in to help lead the way to complete reformation.

Seeing **O** and **K** rolling in, Capital **F** called to them with his newfound flourish,
"Well hello, **O** and **K**; you look fit as two fiddles! Where have you been?"

"We've made our way back to Dim's mean streets
after emerging from the *Dictionary of Deletes*," explained **O**.

"What's that?" asked **w**.

"The dictionary contains concepts we need to know," explained Big **O**.
"It lists words and their meanings."

Leaning in with great interest, **T** asked, "What did you learn?"

"We learned where we came from and who we are,
and that each of us is perfect without blemish or scar."

"So gather 'round," instructed Coach **K**. "We've got a lot to say."

(Even "kill-joy" **j** turned his jot in the direction of **K**.)

A hush greeted **K** as she announced, "Folks, it's all been a hoax."

"We've never been Debtors," said **O**. "It was a bad joke that we believed.
A debtor life is nothing that Be would conceive."

"Then how did this farce begin?" asked **A**.

"And is there an end?" asked **Z**.

"Let me tell you about our genesis."

"What's that?"

"How we came to be," answered **T**. "Please continue."

Accordingly, **O** and **K** beckoned their friends to listen as their genesis was retold.

"In the Beginning is Being, and Being is all there is.
And Being beams bright and calls itself Be.
And Be was, and is, and always will be good, because good is Be's reality."

The letters listened carefully with attention, intension, and retention.

"So is there Be and **B**?" asked **F**, confessing some confusion.

"Yes," answered **O**. "Remember, Be is short for Being, and Being is everywhere we are.
We can't be without Being."

"That's logical," replied **T**, "because we can't be outside of Being."

"And if **B** resides in Being, she can reappear here," concluded Little **o**.

"Correct!" stated Coach **K**. "**B**, whom you believed was erased,
will reappear as you realize Be's creation can not be effaced."

"Then, we each must eradicate any belief
that good can ever descend into grief," shouted **c**.

"I'm willing to do that," volunteered **p**, "because it redeems the power that I gave to **D**."

And everyone happily agreed with **p**.

"The Law of Good is simple and grand," stated **O** confidently.
"Be supplies when we demand."

"Let's take our stand, and demand to see **B** right here," shouted **p**.

"Let's begin at the very Beginning," sang **c** with her whole heart and soul.

So they all got quiet, closed their eyes, and began to eradicate every belief that had accepted
the false premise and conclusion that error was true.

And quite frankly, dear reader, they each had much remedial work to do.

They remained in this state until each individual letter honestly and consciously
had removed every erroneous view suggesting **B**'s demise.

And then, to their surprise, when they opened their eyes,
B was standing in their midst, beaming her benevolent and beautiful smile,
which seemed to extend for mile upon mile.

"Thank you, each friend," sang **B** ever so sweetly, "for putting an end to the belief that Life
can be brief. For as you can see in me, Be's 'beginning' lasts forever."

"Then goodness never ends?" asked **Z**. "There is no interruption?"

"That's right," affirmed **B**. "How can there be Being without Be and **B**?
Beginning remains intact because lack has no beginning, so it can never attack."

"So, goodness applies to you . . . and me . . . and, oh my gosh . . . **D**?" gasped **Z**.

156

B nodded in agreement.

"Then we've got to free **D** from our incorrect view," cried **E**.

"We must *un*see the diabolical **D**," offered **Z**.

"We must strip **D** of his bogus power," stated **p**.

"And refuse to deify error or terror from this very hour," cried **q**.

"Can we do this?" interjected **j**. "What about Hate and the price that we'll pay?"

B replied, "There's nothing to fear, because goodness is here.
Won't you join us, **j**?"

But **j** just turned toward the gray.

"**j**, please stay. Why go astray?" urged **B**.

"Why not?" retorted **j**, as he went on his solitary way.

"Have patience," called **K** to the others, breaking the funk.
"**j** just has to deal with some split-personality junk."

The letters gazed sadly as **j** disappeared into the haze of Un's perpetually gray day.

Now, for the first time, the remaining lowercase letters
consistently strived for capitalization.
While there were some successes, there were challenges, too.

"Here's an idea," said **U**.
"Why don't we unite to help each other when we're tempted to moan
or feel all alone."

"Good idea," said **S**, "like a studio where we practice the art of being single-minded."

"Let's call it *The Gathering Whole*," suggested **c**.

"Where will it be?" asked **w**.

"Wherever we have a meeting of the minds," suggested **B**. "That way it's practical."

Thus, *The Gathering Whole* came to be
quite the site for growth, confession,
light, and expression.

For example, Little **o** asked Big **O** one day,
"How do you grow into a big omni-O from a little, undersized **o** like me?"

"What makes you think you're undersized?"

"Compared to you, I really fall short . . . "

Then, Big **O** interrupted to sing this retort:

"Omni means ALL. It's the essence of good,
Governing everyone's being in Be's Omni-hood.
This essence inspires all that we do;
You just need to perceive it to let it shine through.

"You'll find it all there in your original heart;
It's always been in you right there from the start."

"Oh no," winced **o**.
"I've limited, compared, and judged myself all wrong;
now I'd better start whistling my individual song . . .
and Big **O**, would you like to whistle along?"

Opening up, **o** whistled a duet with Big **O**,
and the duo put on a magnificent show.
All the others joined them and beat right along,
and before he knew it, **o**'s lowercase image was gone.

O's big heart was now quadrupled in size,
and he found himself standing shoulder to shoulder with Big **O** — all capitalized!

They then took their places as the Double O Agents in "gOOd,"
as **c**, weeping happily, capitalized, as a self-less **C** would.

It was interesting to note that, though the **O**'s looked the same,
each maintained his uniqueness, and an individual name.
They dropped "big" and "little" with their tittles and jots,
and chose virtuous names,
like Good-Work and Good-Thoughts.

"This is a big day," said Good-Thoughts **O**, no longer a tot.
"Thank you, Be. I'm grateful. I'm grateful a lot."

"You're welcome," laughed Be — invisible, but right there on the spot.

And from his bleak and unhappy haunts, **D** resented the joyful renaissance.

"there'll be hell to pay for this," he hissed, all alone in the gloom.
"yes, there'll be hell to pay, but when . . . and by whom?"

Chapter 39

DETACHMENT

Done

"but when . . . and by whom?" repeated **D**, yelling in his self-created cell.

"but when . . . and by whom?" he cried, trembling.
"i can feel **B** lowering the boom,
burying me in an unforgiving tomb.

"**B** is haunting me!
taunting me!
flaunting her glee
that i'll be nothing —
nothing but Debris.

"i erased her by my will, but that still didn't kill her.
she's probably near and is bound to appear.
oh Dear! i am about to realize my very worst fear.

"my fate has been controlled by that incubus, Hate!
i've been stung and hung out to Die," he cried.
"stung! stung! stung to Death,
but why?"

In the deepest and darkest recesses of Deadquarters,
D hunkered down, depressed and distressed,
expecting that he'd be the one to have to pay
for the letters' liberation, enjoyment, and play.

Pouting, **D** complained, "they're having fun, while i'm stung here in un."

"Fun?" questioned Hate, hovering unseen in the bleak dankness of **D**'s fate.
"Well then, do something hateful and absurd.
Fun is an awful, unacceptable word."

But, refusing to be used, **D** began his revolt,
screaming, "i am not your Dolt!"

This rebellion infuriated Hate,
who flew into an irate frenzy.

Searching for something to say that would scare **D** back into compliance,
Hate snorted, "**D**, you're Debilitated and Debunked!"

"go ahead and berate me, but i'm Done biting your bait!"

"You're weak," mocked Hate, "still weak!
Poor little **D** is too weak to squeak.
You're afraid, and you'll be undone,
when I go and blab it all over Un!"

D's suspicion had yielded fruition.

It was now apparent that he would be the one
to pay for the letters' newfound way to freedom.

With defiance, **D** declared, "i told you, get another Decoy,
'cause i'm Done with your ploy."

Sensing a rout, it was Hate's turn to pout.

"Aw, come on, **D**, you know I'm nothing without you," entreated Hate, trying to coax **D** back
into service.

"i'm Done in un," said **D**.
"you and those Dumb Debtor-letters can't accuse or abuse me anymore."

"Well . . . um . . . ah . . . ," stammered Hate, trying to think fast. "**D**, we're a team, and <u>we</u>
may not be revered, but I have a new weapon that <u>will</u> be revered and feared!"

"yeah, well, whatever," muttered **D**.

With mounting frustration, Hate commenced
a verbal rampage of foul obscenities,
perverse curses,
and inane four-letter words,
culminating in a crescendo of outrageous expletives
restating Hate's unabating vow.

"I, Hate, shall annihilate Be's State of Being."

But, in spite of this proclamation with its deviant oration,
D was unmoved.

Judging the situation, Hate deduced,
"**D** is useless, but I won't let go of control!"

Demanding that negativity take its toll,
Hate paused, then cried,
"Wait! Kill-joy **j** and 'the beast' will be my aces-in-the-hole."

And off went Hate to feed his inner beast, while tempting fate — alone.

Chapter 40

DYSFUNCTION

The Beast

Evil's disappearance and **D**'s defection were indeed serious setbacks.

However, Hate had suspected all along that the Beta-beat could only achieve
capitalization through 100% unification,
so it searched in the gray for **j**,
until it caught the scent of his detachment and vulnerability.

"If just one Beta-beat letter is destroyed," reasoned Hate,
"or, better yet, self-destroyed,
my dream of negating good will come true.
What fun will ensue as I break **j** in two."

Sniffing his presence, Hate chanted:
"I demand the impressionable **j** appear. **j** will answer my command.
I insist, and nothing can resist what I have planned.
And when he comes, I'll stalk, then sting, and . . . "

But Hate stopped and gaped right there,
as its responsive bait bounced into his lair.

"Say, **j**, you're looking out of joint," whispered Hate,
aware that **j** was at a crucial junction in his juvenile dysfunction.

j retorted, "My jot's hot and my hook's gettin' cooked."

"Sounds like a 'we-lationship' problem," wheezed Hate, happy to see **j**'s precarious state.

"I'm sick of life," he blared, avoiding Hate's mesmeric stare.

"Stick with me, **j**, and we'll capsize that capitalized crew," squeezed Hate,
oozing forth a thick, stinking goo
that immediately engulfed **j** in sticky-icky lies and untruths.

Struggling fiercely, **j** pleaded, "I can't move in all this goo."

Then, with its true gooey-evil identity revealed, Hate demanded, "Worship me, **j**!"

Well, **j**'s jot was getting hotter than hot, and his hook instinctively yelped, "Help!"

But as far as he could look,
j could only see gook.

With no help in sight, and now incapacitated, hypnotized, and hopeless,
j closed his jot,
praying Hate's negations would stop.

But they didn't.

Instead, Hate whispered, "Repeat after me: 'Feed the Beast.'"

Feebly, **j** repeated, "Feed the beast."

"Again!" demanded Hate. "Louder!"

"Feed the Beast?" whimpered **j**.

"More!" snarled Hate.

"Feed the Beast. Feed the Beast," uttered the petrified **j**.

With each repetition,
Hate gradually morphed into a beastly apparition.

Lusting with pride and swelling inside,
Hate soon mutated into

The Beast.

There, in the heart of Un, stood a gigantic, reddened, revolting corpus
of
error, greed, hypocrisy, lust, rage, and revenge.

(This Beast was definitely up to no good!)

Chapter 41

IMPROVEMENT

Spite

Meanwhile, the Beta-beat, unaware of **j**'s dilemma, was approaching
COMPLETE CAPITALIZATION.
Their desire to serve Be fired and inspired them constantly
to. higher heights of being.

But, in spite of their progress, the gap between good and bad
was widening into a cataclysmic chasm.

The state of Un was unraveling for sure.

None of this was lost on the Beta-beat letters,
and, as **C** contemplated this wide divide, she confided,
"Any good concept that includes the letter **D**
cannot align to Be's perfect degree."

"Why?" asked **p**.

"Because **D** refuses to capitalize the first letter in each sentence."

"**D** is a real pain," pouted **p**.

"Abstain from complaining," cautioned **M**.

"**M** is correct," stated **T**. "Complaint is a plague."

"I beg to differ with you," defended **q**, siding with **p**.

"Let's reason with **D** and see what he'll do," suggested **U**.

"No way, not me," said **w**.

"Why are you afraid?" asked **x**.

"**D**'s too complex," she answered.

"There's might in many," encouraged **x**. "Let's go together."

"Good idea!" shouted Coach **K**. "Let's go right away."

Accordingly, the Beta-beat, with the exception of **j**, lined up in alphabetical order and marched to **D**'s Deadquarters with conviction.

Here's a depiction:

A B C E F G h I K L M N O p q r S T U V w x Y and **Z**

They marched with precision, looking real tall,
until they saw the Dead-beats killing Time on the mall.

Observing the Dead-beats beating up one of **D**'s guys,
the letters stopped and gawked with suspicious surprise.

"Hey, watch it," shouted Time, waving its clock-like hands at the Dead-beats
to shoo them away.

But the blind assault went on
as the Dead-beats continued to waste Time.

Getting really ticked off, Time beckoned,
"Hey, you Debtors! Don't just stand there;
give me a hand.
These dumb Dead-beats don't know who I am."

"We're beating you up 'cause we know you're corrupt," shouted a Dead-beat.

Down on its hands, Time pleaded to the letters,
"Would you guys mind helping for a second, so I can unwind?"

Alert to the deadly distraction of Time-bound action, **E** cautioned,
"Don't get wound up with Time!
Its face is a fraud! Don't make it a god!"

Awed, the letters huddled together,
wanting to know more.

"An hour has no power to limit or aid.
Stick with Eternity and you won't be delayed."

"**E**, you speak from personal experience," acknowledged **x**.
"You have seen Eternity."

"Yes, I learned that Eternity emancipates; Time divides," confirmed **E**.

"Let's repeal Time," shouted **T**.

"No!" shouted Time, beginning to panic as the unrelenting Dead-beats continued to pile on.

As its hands spun faster and faster trying to scrape the Dead-beats off, Time scoffed,
"This is unfair and criminal,
because my effects are merely subliminal!"

Unimpressed, the letters stared at Time, who glared back, confessing,
"Evil got its upheaval all right,
leaving the Cartel and me wound up real tight.
Well, so much for us and our deadly, dark night;
I must blast into the past, and escape now from sight."

Knowing that Eternity would eventually terminate every time-bound belief,
Time chose relief, and with a wave of its hand, vanished.

"So much for Time and its alarm," shouted **E**. "It can do us no harm.
Let's proceed to Deadquarters."

Hearing the commotion, **D** peeked out his window
to view the crew of overpowering Caps.
Upon seeing **B** with them,
D, shrinking in horror, appeared to collapse.

Then, pulling himself together with a mix of indignation and pain,
D crawled into his corner, reprising his "Bad Song" refrain:

"i'm so bad, i'm Despicable.
i'm Destructively predictable.
i'm cruel, harsh, Deceitful, and vicious.
to sum it up: i'm Deliciously malicious."

Then, he began again.

166

"i'm so bad . . ."

But **x**'s confident knock on his door rocked **D**'s delusion.

"go away; this is my place," sniveled **D**.
Then, peeking out at **B** and the Caps, he relapsed, crying,
"i refuse to be used or abused by **B**!"

"But we need you, **D**.
Unmask your disguise," called **x**.

"oh, really!" **D** sneered with total distrust,
and then de-capitalized out of spite and disgust!

"No!" cried **w**, staring at the lowercase **d**. "Now it's hopeless."

"Don't be hypnotized, **w**," cautioned **x**, as **d** began to drone,
"go ahead, look down on me and see if I'll budge,
'cause it's cozy down here in my Dank, Darkened grudge."

"Maintain our moral high ground," advised **x** to the letters.

"This isn't our concern," cautioned **C**. "It's between **d** and **B**."

"And Be," stated **B** calmly with compassion.

"Yes," agreed **F**. "Remain focused on good,
and ignore the distractions of *could*, *would*, and *should*."

"Yes, **F**, that is x-cellent advice.
When you keep your cool,
you'll never be a fool," declared **X**,
unaware that his moral stand had achieved capital status.

"Wow!" exclaimed **w**, examining the renewed Capital **X**.
"Who knows? Maybe I'll be next."

Chapter 42

Inside Out

Though exhilarated by **X**'s transformation,
the letters were saddened by **d**'s self-imposed degradation.

"Let's depart for *The Gathering Whole*.
I think we should focus on the meaning of soul," suggested **X**.

So, they filed out of Deadquarters one by one,
leaving **d** "undone" in his devolutionary abode.

As the days progressed,
the letters were in an evolutionary mode,
rising higher and higher in thought,
striving to be carefully taught —
not the corrupt ways of **d**,
but about their original, true identity.

To aid in their growth, **E** posted a post
for everyone to remember:

CAPS ARE FOREVER — WITH <u>NEVER</u> A LAPSE.

Reading **E**'s post, **w** conceded, "My understanding has too many gaps.
I don't want to be a lowercase bore anymore.
Would you teach me, please, **T**?"

So **T**, who saw all things transparently,
began teaching **w**
how to translate seen objects into unseen ideas.

"What's an 'idea'?" asked **w**.

"An 'idea' is something seen in thought," instructed **T**.

"You mean, it's an image?"

"It's a thought you can see with your 'inside' eye," replied **T**.

"Can anyone else see it?" asked **w**.

"Not at first, but if you claim it as your thought and nourish it, that idea can become a visible image that represents that thought."

"Like a reflection?"

"Right. A reflection mirrors the original idea perfectly."

"But what if there's a defect in the reflection?" asked **w**.

"Then the defect must be detected and corrected," instructed **T**.

"So if I see a defect on the outside, I must perfect my thought inside."

"Right again, my friend.
What you're seeing on the inside is what will be seen on the outside."

"So if I'm mixing good and bad on the inside, the outside will need fixing."

"Yes; a defective thought always produces a defective effect.
That's why every thought must begin with a good premise, so you get a good conclusion."

"Are you sure the outside always reflects the inside?" asked **w** with reservation.

"Why not find out for yourself?" suggested **T**.
"Just let an outside appearance lead you to ask about the inside thought."

"Ok, I'll start right away," said **w**.

"And remember," added **T**,
"you can only exude a capital image outside, if you first include it inside."

Just then, **X**, coming to study **E**'s post, joined the tandem.

Winking at **T**, **w** asked, "What's up, Big **X**? You look perplexed."

"I am, **w**; thanks for noticing."

"What's up?" asked **w** with sincerity.

"I feel **d** must escape from his self-induced tomb.
And with our help, I know he can elude its dark, painful doom."

"Why should we even care about **d**?
He seems like a lost cause to me," stated **w**.

T reiterated softly to **w**, "Remember, inside determines outside."

"Yes, thank you, **T**," replied **w**, grateful for the reminder.
"How can we help **d** escape his fate?"

X continued, "To save **d**, we must see Be's original **D**."

"So . . . seeing the ideal **D** is the key to his reappearing?" asked **w**.

"Yes," said **X**, "and I feel **d**'s delivery is nearing."

"Why?"

"I sense **d** wants *belief relief.*"

"What's that?"

"Relief from every negative belief that has been governing his thought."

"When will this happen?" asked **w**.

"Soon," replied **X**.

"You'll know that moment with great precision,"
predicted **w**, aware of **X**'s keen x-ray vision.

With these new notions in mind,
w went off by herself to
think, rethink, and think some more.

Before long, **w** declared to **T**, "I think I get it.
The key is to realize the unseen ideal,
then replace what's defective with what's real — and continuous."

"That's the deal," answered **T**. "Now do it with zeal."

"From now on, I'm demanding to see the ideal — even if it kills me!" vowed **w**,
with newfound conviction.

"Seeing the ideal is not only evolutionary, it's revolutionary thinking," affirmed **T**.

"What does 'revolutionary' mean?"

"Revolution is the way to progress from the old to the new.
It's a natural process, the key to a more uplifted view.

"Sometimes it's easy — painless and free.
But more often, it results from a struggle — which can be hard to begin,
yet it's worth it, 'because 'to struggle' is the root of the triumphant word *win*!"

"Thanks, **T**," said **w**, with an inside-outside grin.

Chapter 43

| THE STRUGGLE |

Self-less

"enough, enough," cried **d**, as his Deadquartered grudge
grew and grew into a stew of mental sludge.

"i'm being punished for my evil plot,
and this terrorizing nightmare will never, ever stop.
i've got to escape," he cried.

But then he shivered,
"i'm just too bad to be Delivered
from the hell of this self-imposed cell.
Hate betrayed me — it used me to subvert Be —,
but now nothing is left, just an empty Decree."

Drowning in remorse, **d** droned in a monotone:

"i was bad, Despicable,
Destructive, and predictable.
i was cruel, harsh, Deceitful, and vicious.
now, in the end, i'm nothing — fictitious."

Totally derailed, **d** wailed and wailed,
"i have made a terrible, Despicable choice."

Then, he lost what was left of his voice.

But, undeterred, he lamented on,
"because Be is good, i chose to be bad;
. . . and biggest, I chose to be bad; . . . and strongest, i *chose* to be bad.

171

"Hate said i was weak,
but i was afraid to be weak,
so i chose to be *bad*."

And so very, very sad, **d** wept.

"then my belief in bad tried to hide Be,
which is impossible, 'cause Be can't even be seen.
why, why, why Did i voice that Deceptive concept called 'choice'?"

Unconsolable, **d** paced in his crippling mental space, whining,
"i want relief from this grief.
but i know now that Be is in the heart of all who will agree,
and i sort of wish *i* had even a wee bit of Be in me.
but i am no good, a real good-for-nothing **d**,
because i have betrayed Be, the Alpha-beat . . . *and me*."

Then, he whispered in a hushed, raspy tone,
"there's no way *up* for me, but there is a way *out*."

And at that fatal moment, **d** whispered, "i have had enough!"

So, out he went to find a way to end his day . . . forever.

~ ~ ~

At that precise moment, **X** exclaimed, "**w**, let's make a trek to visit **j**."

"Ok," said **w** warily, "but you know **j** has the blues."

"Low spirits with blue notes?"

"Yup."

"This isn't good news," responded **X**. "Let's go."

Immediately, they ventured into the gray to find the melancholy **j**.
And it was a very good thing that they journeyed that day.

After a while, **X**, with its ear to the ground, whispered, "Do you hear that bubbling sound?"

Frowning, **w** whispered,
"It's coming from 'round the bend.
I sure hope it's not a 'dead' end."

"We must proceed with caution," whispered **X**. "Follow me."

Rounding the bend, the friends were upended
by a debilitating scene, turning **w**'s innards a sickening green.

Here's the picture:

Gushing from **j**'s hot, swollen jot
was a lava-like goo of despotic inflammation
infected with The Beast's dualistic adoration.

j's demented jot,
crazed from being so gooey hot,
was expanding into a hole
and coaxing **d** to jump in!

Alone, and void of all delight, **d** was preparing to dive.

The hot jot cajoled, "Don't fear or doubt.
When you jump in, you'll no longer be out."

d was fascinated by the force of the mesmerizing jot.

"Darkness is light; to be wrong is your right!
Death is a delight. Come, jump in out of sight," continued the captivating jot.

"Death can save me," reiterated **d**. "Death is an answer, but is it the key?"

Uncertain whether to jump in or not,
d peered deeper and deeper
into the fiery lava of **j**'s suggestive jot,
increasingly seduced by the goo on its spot.

The heartbeats of **w** and **X** began to increase, seeing the likelihood of **d**'s imminent decease.

"**d**'s hesitating," whispered **X**. "Get ready to grab him."

173

The ever-growing jot, all slathered and hot, cooed hypnotically,
"Come on, **d**. Stop feeling queasy.
Come, jump right on in. It's all so easy.
Come on, just do it. There's really nothing to it!"

"nothing," sighed **d**.
"nothing is the something that I want to be."
Then **d** began mumbling, "i am nothing. i am nothing," teetering dangerously toward the
ever-expanding hole.

Meanwhile, **X**, whose capitalized **X**-ray vision could now penetrate
the state of all things,
began to earnestly examine **d**'s soul,
as he tottered there, dangerously close to death's seductive sinkhole.

Suddenly, **X** proclaimed with brilliant insight,
"In the beginning, **D** was conceived by Be's delight,
and what begins in that light remains perpetually bright."

"Right!" shouted **w**.

"This **D** is exempt from separation, frustration, and annihilation," declared **X** emphatically.

Thus, seeing **d**'s life in its original conception,
X proclaimed, "**d** is whole, composed of incorruptible perfection."

"Whole?" asked **w**.

"This **d** definitely is not what he seems," proclaimed **X**.
"His real identity is what Being beams.
The outward appearance is only a ruse,
brought on by the notion that life's ours to lose."

"Whole?" responded the eavesdropping **j**.
"I want to be whole in the very worst way."

Now **j**'s hook, hearing the results of **X**'s **X**-ray look,
sought to disengage his jot from the confounding gook.

The hook grabbed the jot and held on real tight,
while The Beast, lurking nearby within sight,
buzzed wildly, adding to **j**'s plight.

174

Alarmed by The Beast's buzz, **X** bellowed, "Let go of the jot."

"No, I cannot!" hollered **j**.

"Why?"

"My jot is jovial and much overjoyed,
and without it, everyone's joy just might be destroyed."

"But you're not responsible for our joy," countered **X**.

"Joy's not in one spot or alone in a jot," cried **w**.

"I'm so hot," gasped **j**, beginning to wheeze.
"Something is trying to seize control of my soul."

Suddenly, rising from the misty gray, The Beast's giant hulk materialized.

Roaring fiercely, The Beast cried,
"I will rule to the death everything that draws breath.
Idolize me and my sting, for I, The Beast, am now your King."

Manically, it turned on **d** and began to sting
with its barbed harpooning-tail-kinda-thing.

"yeow!" screamed **d** with a shrill, "it's trying to kill my soul!"

Pushed from behind by The Beast, and in a stupor from the sting,
d was propelled toward the jot, singing a death-curdling, "yes!"

"No!" wailed **w**.

But it was too late to negate the sting,
as **d** was sucked into the gooey ring
of **j**'s jot —
an expanding black spot; death's final resting plot.

"Wait," shouted **w**. "Wait!

This beast of death and hate has no right to determine our fate!"
"I have the power to negate the hole by giving my 'w' to save d's soul."

Then, without wavering, and with saving d as her goal,
w cannonballed deep into the jot's poisonous hole.

~ ~ ~

Concurrently, as w jumped into the hole to rescue d,
the airborne Beast lunged at ɹ's hook, buzzing rapaciously.
Its bulging thighs overpowered the wheezing ɹ,
squeezing him tight and lifting him up and away.

~ ~ ~

The instant w plunged into the unknowing depth,
she felt the breadth and the might of Be's immortal light.

Leaning on this peace,
which increased as she continued her descent,
w had never felt more empowered or content.

"Your life is in me," sang Be.

"I agree," sang w, fearless and free.

"Promise you'll always love d," continued Be.

"I will," promised w.

And then it was still.

~ ~ ~

That is, until ɹ's hook, filled with terror in mid-air,
spoke up while peering down on the others with increasing despair.

"What are you going to do?' asked ɹ, feeling the anguish of being separated from his jot.

"Let's just say your lot is to remain torn in two," tormented The Beast in flight.

"What will happen to me, and **w**, and **d**?" asked ⅃, fearing their plight.

"This has been one heck of a night.
w and **d** are already dead, and you have just lost your head.
But don't worry, ⅃, there's lots to do before I begin . . . to chew."

"Chew?" cried ⅃ in horror.

"That's right, chew on you."

"No!" screamed ⅃, as The Beast stung it with its flailing tail of poison and lust.

"I'm disgusting," smirked The Beast, winging its way to the Dis-animation Station
with ⅃ in tow.

~ ~ ~

As The Beast disappeared from sight,
w was in awe at the immediacy of her might.

You see, giving both her spirit and her letter had annulled the attack,
imploding the hole, and ejecting **d**
and Capital **W** —
unearthed, re-birthed, and wholly intact.

Whistling, **X** exclaimed, "Holy Alpha-beat, **W**! You really took action."

Taken aback, **W** gasped, "Today, I acted first!"

And then she explained, in a kind of confessional verse:
"Safe, safer, safest was my position of choice.
It's no wonder I wavered, always losing my voice.
I worried, ruminated, and wondered a lot —
quibbled and questioned, scared to leave my safe spot.

"So, always poised to react,
I never dreamed I could annul an attack.
Taking a stand — today is a first.
Wow, acting's the best and reacting's the worst."

"You're the Queen, **W**, and that is a fact," exclaimed **X**,
giving a high five and getting one back.

"What's the word, Your Highness?"

"Be told me to love **d**, and I agreed," she whispered.

Then, appraising **d**'s physique, lying comatose and weak,
W responded from the very depth of her core,
"The delusion is no more.
And now, I'll care for our neighbors like never before."

           W and **X** christened that desire with silence.

That is, until **W** gasped, "What happened to ♩?"

"That beast took it up and away."

Chapter 44

METAMORPHOSIS

The Malice Palace

    While in flight with ♩ as its captive, The Beast grew delirious with hunger.

    Having consumed nothing since he morphed into The Beast,
the former Hate craved a delectable feast.

    It flew to its lair in the creepy heart of Dim,
where the blinking sign above the saloon doors read,
"The Malice Palace — Living For The Dead."

    There, ♩ was dumped at the Dis-Animation Station
to await future examination.

    The Beast swaggered into the Palace mess hall,
drooling at the thought of ♩'s carcass, hook and all.

"I should have devoured ♩ while I could," complained the brute.
"Now I have nothing, and I'm ravenous to boot.

"How much time, I wonder, will it take . . . to bake . . . ♩?"

    Suddenly, from out of the gray, Time materialized.

"Can I help you?" smiled The Beast, sizing up Time's meal appeal.

Appraising The Beast for the first time, Time was dumbstruck and scared to death.

Finally, under his breath, Time, very fluttered, muttered, "Where's Hate?"

"You're too late, Time," roared The Beast with gluttonous glee.

"As you can see, Hate has morphed into — me!"

"Oh, I see," whimpered Time, ticking erratically.

"Wanna feast?"

"Feast on wha . . . wha . . . what?" stuttered Time, now sweating blood.

"On you, stud. I'm about to nip you in the bud!"

Terrified, Time lapsed, then collapsed into a smattering
of seconds, minutes, and hours scattered all over the floor.

"Oh . . . uh . . . say no more," buzzed Time with great alarm. "Mind you, no harm."

With titillating taste buds, The Beast surveyed the immensity of Time, sighing,
"This unexpected banquet of Time will surely be, at least, sublime."

"What a crime," howled Time, kowtowing on the floor.

"You're such a bore," roared the ravenous Beast.
"And now it's time to feast!"

Expecting a savory blend of flavors,
The Beast ran its huge, red tongue over every nanosecond of Time.
But with each lap, its enthusiasm for Time was zapped.

Suddenly realizing that its "feast" had neither substance, flavor, nor savor,
The Beast spit it out, howling, "This is a crime!
"I'm craving to taste, but I'm just wasting Time."

Thus, Time's demise was postponed,
and, feeling abused and alone, it excused itself with haste.

"This imposter, Time, has no taste! It's an utter disgrace taking up space!
I need substance — I want more," The Beast roared.

Famished, The Beast began ransacking the deserted mess hall for something sweet to eat.

Eventually, its eyes fell on an enticing treat:
the *Up-To-No-Good Cookbook*.

"This ought to show Me how to prepare ⅃ and its hook," laughed The Beast.
"On this feast night, I'll finally taste Be's Alpha-beat delight."

Drooling, The Beast began to imagine amputating ⅃'s hook.

Upon scanning the book, its beady eyes fell on a recipe,
arousing it into a state of carnivorous ecstasy.
A pernicious recipe lay there on the pages,
with noxious words from out of the ages!

"To cook a hook,
look here," it read.

"Sever with neglect, then infect with will,
criticize till near death, then, suck out its breath."

"Ah yes, this yummy recipe will eradicate Be's creation forever," roared The Beast.

"Without ⅃, Be's entire design will crack,
and I, formerly known as Hate, will have what Hate always lacked:

BEASTLY SUPREMACY.

"Finally, Be's Language of Life will be negated by Me,
and My Kingdom of Strife — realized —
will forever be . . . sensationalized, mesmerized, and supremely super-sized!

"With no good words, there will be no good works.
Hypocrisy will prevail, while law and order fail.
Chaos will be mine and pandemonium will rule,
with malice governing all as my unseen tool.

"Let's see," droned The Beast. "I'll choose pain as My pleasure
and whip up the poison, measure for measure."

Having memorized the recipe from the cookbook, The Beast began chanting,
"Poison, fill Me now with malicious ill will —
noxious nega-tudes that negate, maim, and kill;
greed, envy, pride, and spite, selfishness, anger — My numbing delight."

With manners gluttonous and crude,
The Beast then swallowed every negative 'tude.
Salivating, it savored each malodorous morsel,
until an obnoxious stench belched from the down-under of its torso.

"Pee-yew, this is so bad, it's good," spewed The Beast. "At least, this will last for a while."

Fortunately, that putrefied stench quenched the brute's immediate desire for ⌐.

"I think everything is going My way," declared The Beast with a yawn.
"I am the King, and ⌐ is My pawn."

Then, self-indulged and smug, the inebriated slug
fell asleep on the mess hall rug.

~ ~ ~

Now, when ⌐ had been dumped at the Dis-Animation Station,
dark, frigid air had suspended his animation.

Stuck in the freezer, on the very top shelf,
he found he could at least still talk to himself.

The dialogue, however, was going nowhere
until the memory of The Beast grabbed him foursquare.

"Help!" he yelped, frozen there all alone.

And that cry, with its heart-opening tone, raised ♩ up into a groovy kind of zone.

There, in spite of his icicled physique,
Be's calming thought dawned upon him, "You can still think."

This was a new thought for ♩.

"Hey, I <u>can</u> still think. Say, why don't I replace a cold thought
with a new one that's groovy and hot."

♩ determined, right then and there, to review his journey into despair.

"When and how did I fall?" he wondered. And then, slowly, ♩ began to recall . . .
"I used to be free-spirited, a truly jubilant ♩,
but then a label disabled and reversed my joy one day.

"I thought I was beaming joy — j-o-y —, but, annoyed, **D** saw it reversed as y-o-j.

"So, 'backwards ♩' **D** called me, last instead of first.
Is it any wonder I wandered from good, to bad, to worst?

"Then everyone rehearsed that curse into a habit,
and I've had it for so long.
Now I see that this label hushed, then flushed my joyous song."

Crushed by the weight of his blues, ♩ wept.

Hot, angry tears flowed out of his spout,
making way for better thoughts, which then had room to sprout.

Gradually, a revelation dawned, as ♩ realized right out loud:
"A habit disables, with a label believed to be a law,
which sentences its believer with a fictitious, fatal flaw.

"I employed those labels: ill, dis, im, mis, un, mal, ob;
but now, those days are done 'cause I am quittin' that job."

Then, ⌐ disabled every negative label.

That all-night, mental workout melted the gooey web of fright,
and suddenly ⌐ cried, "Hey, I'm free; and jeepers, **O** and **K** were right!
I'm fired up and able, and I'll be livin' label-free,
so I'm boppin' outta here, and I'm gonna stick with Be."

Hence, finally getting the point, ⌐ blew out of that unhappenin' joint.

Stirred by the sound of ⌐'s escape, the startled Beast awoke with a quake.

Instinctively, it released a fetid flood of crud in the form of blackened vocabulary phlegm,
condemning his hook with, "You're cooked, ⌐."

Lumbering feverishly amidst its flood of crud,
The Beast was advancing and hungry for blood.

Just when it looked like the end was near,
Be's invisible arms just seemed to appear.
Feeling the embrace of those mighty arms,
⌐ grabbed on to escape The Beast's impending harm.

Those loving arms balanced ⌐, lifting him up and away.
Then, when all was steady, they released the capitalized **J**.

Lifted above The Beast's River of Wrong,
J was jubilating a liberation song.
For from the instant he had permitted his soul to fly,
J began singing "Joyrider in the Sky."

He soared, sang, and signed good words in the sky.

Then **A**, hearing a song, cried, "Look, way up high!"

"Hey," laughed **Z**, zooming a sonic, "Hooray!
That's our joy-friend and neighbor, Be's Capital **J**."

So, **Z** threw a party and they all danced away.
They tripped the light fantastic — especially **Y**, **Z**, **A**, and **J**.

Reformation

As the faint beam of light began rising just over the hill,
W and **X** trekked in carrying **d**, corpse-like and still.

The remaining partiers who had stayed gathered 'round,
stared as **d** was laid tenderly down on the ground.

"Where in Un have you been?" asked **q** with chagrin. "I was worried."

"We've had quite a day," exclaimed **X**.

"And behold **W**," extolled **B**. "We should all give her a capital-sized hug!"

And that's exactly what the exuberant letters did,
nearly squeezing **W** into a V!

"Whee," giggled **W**. "It's so good to be here."

"What have you learned?" asked **T**, shedding a tear,
while embracing his pupil with an extra special hug.

"I learned that **d** is our sibling; he isn't a thug."

"I don't mean to be smug," piped up **p**, "but who is your source?"

"Be."

Silence.

"Then what shall we do?" asked **q**, staring down at **d**.

"Like **W**, we must correct our view," declared **U**.

"Correct *our* view?" spewed **q** with pent-up resentment.
"Why should we change?
D defamed, blamed, and maimed us from the beginning.
He should be punished, not helped!"

"That's all in the past; and besides, it wasn't his fault," explained **B**, jumping to **d**'s defense.

(It was a good thing, because that moment was tense!)

"**d** was stung, deluded, confused, and used by the Cartel to fulfill their plan.
Demanding punishment can't right wrongs;
it just enthrones error, which leads to more terror.
d must reform his norm," stated **B** confidently.

"This makes sense, and it's pragmatic, too," responded **p**.

"Well then, if **d** belongs to Be, I repeat, what should we do?" demanded **q**.

"We must correct our incorrect view," affirmed **p** quietly to **q**.

"How do I do that?" asked **q** in a quandary, confessing,
"I admit I've been infected with hate."

"Reject it," stated **K**. "Open up your mind
and be very kind to both yourself and **d**."

Agreeing, **T** added, "Affection neutralizes infection."

"Especially the infection called 'delusion,'" confirmed **K**.

"Yes," professed **T**. "We must eradicate all confusion from our conclusions.
I intuit that **O**, **V**, **L**, and **E** hold the key to restoring **d**'s original identity."

"I agree," said **W**, hoping the others would see the real and not the superficial **d**.

Hearing their names,
L, **O**, and **V** stepped forward to join **E**.

Then, **T** advised, "Please retreat to *The Gathering Whole* with Coaches **O** and **K**,
B, **d**, **h**, and me."

"How can I help?" whispered **B** to **T**.

"What's at the root of the word *absolute*?" asked **T**.

"*To set free,*" replied **B**.

"You will be a visible reminder of our Absolute Be — Author of the Law of Freedom."

"That's beautiful," sang **B**. "Thank you, **T**."

185

Inspired at *The Gathering Whole*,
B suggested an idea she called "Free-Form."

"Good idea!" encouraged **K**, assuming the role of coach with **B** and **T**'s blessing.

"What do you mean by Free-Form?" asked **V**.

"Good question," replied **K**, winking at **B** and **T**.
"Free-Form reform occurs with an absolute focus on Be
by understanding its *absolute* root, which is *to set free*."

"You mean, we're completely free from what *seems to be*?"

"That's right, **V**; only then will we see what is true —
the pure and simple, singular view."

"Oh, I see," said **V**. "We must let go of the 'deformed'
before we can be informed of the norm."

"Right!" exclaimed Coach **K**. "That's how we reform."

"**h**, will you hold **d** in your heart
while the rest of us are doing our part?" asked Good-Works **O**.

"Gladly," replied **h**. "I once told **d** that I would be the one who would 'stay' with him,
and that day, I prayed that this day would come."

"You're a good chum," cried **L**. "Now . . . let's not succumb to fear."

"Fear can't appear when we're here at the *Whole*," declared **h**.

"Why?" quizzed **T**, seeing that **h** was on a roll.

"Because there's no hole or crack through which fear can attack."

"Indeed," sang **E**. "*Whole* precludes lack."

"How shall we line up?" asked **L**. "I feel uplifted already."

"How about **EVOL**," suggested Good-Thoughts **O**.

"Good idea," replied Good-Works **O**.
"Keep focused on soul and just let it roll."

And they did just that,
evolving right into the understanding of Being
as pure and perfect
Love.

With uncontrollable joy, Good-Thoughts **O** sang, "Oh, I feel whole,
warm-hearted, wholesome, and free. Wholeness is Love, and it's happening in me!"

"Love is Be," sang **E**, recalling Eternity, "and Be is Love."

"Love's like a song that's singing in me," whispered **V**
with inconceivable serenity.

"I see Love as infinite affection that meets all our needs.
It grows and blossoms from the smallest of seeds," sang **L**.

"Love is transparent," sang **T**. "It's where we begin."

"It's Love that unites us and makes us all kin," sang Good-Works **O**
with an indescribable grin.

"Love showers us with the power of Being," summarized **B**.

"Yes, yes, yes, we have the key,
so scrunch up tightly next to **h** and **d**.
Now we know the way,"
reverently sang the satisfied **K**.

Heeding **K**'s lead, **L**, **O**, **V**, and **E** locked arms and pulled together real tight.

As they did, the humble ensemble was engulfed in a blazing light
of understanding and a compelling need to do what was right.

With the dawning conception of the all-inclusive Be
as being their first and only love,
L, **O**, **V**, and **E** felt the cleansing radiance of Be's perfect gaze,
which removed the sense of **d**'s former gray haze.

Basking within the fresh breeze of ease and delight,
they gleaned that everything is seen
through the love-lens of Be's perfect sight.

Intuitively, they knew that everything was all right,
and agreed they had found the key to capitalizing **d**.

187

Then, the gratified team ratified the

~ Evolve Love Accord ~

— by which they unanimously agreed that Love is living truth.

~ ~ ~

"Forsooth," nodded **Y**, as she quietly passed by *The Gathering Whole*.

"So, when we love each other," reasoned **Y**, "Love will be forever in season."

"Hello, **Y**," called **W**, also out on a walk. "Can we talk?"

"Sure; what's new, **W**?"

"Thanks to you and my new outlook, I have decided to write a book."

"Wonderful, **W**; what's your topic?"

"Freedom and friendship," replied **W**, void of all doubt.

"How so?" asked **Y**.

"I knew the moment **d** and I emerged from **j**'s sinkhole
that I would write about an aspect of Soul."

"Why *freedom* and *friendship*?"

"I investigated the root of the words 'free' and 'friend.'"

"And then?"

"As I looked down at the page from above,
I saw that the root of both words is the same one — 'to love.'"

"So when we all love each other," reasoned **Y**, "we all will be free . . . "

"And together, we will prove this by loving our **d**," concluded **W** with confidence.

"Then there will be no need for offenses or defenses," added **Y**.

"Or negative consequences," agreed **W**, "because we will honestly say what we mean
and mean what we say, inviting each one's expression to elevate the day."

"Best wishes, **W**. I know you have a lot to say," said **Y**, waving good-bye.

"Much more than I knew," sighed the tried-and-true, willing **W**.

Just then, **K** and the crew drew near to make an announcement.

"Listen up," called Coach **K** to the entire Beta-beat.

"What's the plan?" asked **p**.

"To love **d**," sang **L**, **O**, **V**, and **E** in four-part harmony.

"According to the Law of Be, we all must love in order to evolve," added **E**.

"Love must be practical," insisted **U**. "Let's test it and see.
If there's proof, you'll have a believer in me."

They all agreed that if love were practical, they'd see a change in **d**.
So they began refining their plan.

Chapter 46

| TRANSFORMATION |

Forgiven

"Confound those letters," roared The Beast to Fear.
"Why can't you make their zeal disappear?"

"We don't stand a chance against Love," groaned Fear, glancing with dread
at The Beast's ugly head.

"What's love?" asked an attending Dead-beat. "Never heard of that."

"Love annihilates hate," spat The Beast, already in an irate state.

"Translate," whispered one Dead-beat to another.

"Love liberates," it replied.
"Without any fuss, love liberates everyone — everyone but us."

"Silence!" screamed The Beast.
"Fear, command all the Dead-beats to infiltrate and spy,
to help you spread our most powerful lie."

"Which lie is that?" asked Fear nervously.

"That the fear they feel is real!" snapped The Beast.
"Begin now, before it's too late!"

"Oh, great," sighed Fear, wishing it could disappear.

~ ~ ~

A short time later, Capital **I** called, "Gather 'round, everyone, to hear the good news."

They obediently assembled, anticipating something grand.

"Coach **K** will now reveal our *Evolve Love* plan," concluded **I**, standing down as **K** took center stage to thunderous applause.

"Thank you, **I**," sang **K**. "My dear, wholehearted friends,
here are the details of the *Evolve Love Accord*.
First, we'll expose the *bad* words that begin with 'de' and end in disaster."

"But suppose we need the bad words to balance the good?"
suggested the Dead-beat spies, disseminating lies in the neighborhood.

p promptly retorted,
"Like and unlike don't ever equate,
because Un has no presence, power, or weight.
The *ill* logic that 'bad' exists is askew and untrue,
subsisting only through mistakes in thinking by me and by you."

"Impurity is an impossibility," testified **q**,
dismissing the suggestion with,
"No negative is true."

Immediately, those Dead-beat spies and their lies evaporated for good,
while both **P** and **Q** stood capitalized.

For their sudden dismissals of the negative lies,
they had each hit the mark, and both won the prize.

"Before we begin," suggested **h**, "let's put **d** right in the center so he'll feel and know that we love him so. Remember, our Beta-beat won't be complete until **d** is free."

"Good!" said **I**. "First, we'll expose the 'de' vocabulary words that are based on a bad premise."

"I'll start," said **A**, whispering, "Deactivate."

The letters paused, waiting to see if **d** would respond,
but there was no sign of life.

Then **B** whispered, "Debilitate,"

. . . followed by a long pause to contemplate.

Next, **C** whispered,
"Destroy."

"who's calling me?" wondered **d**, responding intuitively to the sound of his name,
as each letter continued to defame subsequent negative concepts.

"Decline."

"who's calling me?" he asked, stirring from his stupor.

"Delay."

"why won't they leave me alone?" he moaned, fighting to regain consciousness.

"Decay."

"please . . . please . . . please . . . go away," he struggled to say.

"Deceive."

"Deflate."

"i hate my fate," he thought, berating himself, now conscious of his surroundings.

"Deteriorate . . ."

"Wait," whispered **W**. "Why are we whispering?"

191

"Because we hate these words," declared **r** spitefully.

"**r**, please stop," cautioned **P**. "Be alert; hate hurts!"

But **r** continued ranting,
"**d** wounded us with his negative words,
and it's absurd for us to just let him go.

"He's guilty, I know, and that is a fact,
because he stung us with every verbal attack.
Loving **d** is just too hard for me.
Who here agrees?"

"I do," cried a few.

"Me, too," added **Q**, reacting instinctively. "**d** shattered our quietude!"

"**d** is guilty, and should be punished for all of his lies," declared **r**.

"they're right," **d** admitted inside, expecting the group to soon thrash his hide.

"Please listen; be still," cautioned **W**. "You sound just like . . . "

"Wait!" whispered **r**, "I sound just like Hate.
Oh my, what an awful mistake!"

And with Capital **R**'s awakening, his lowercase **r** accusations abated
right then and there — for good.

~ ~ ~

Concurrently, a few Dead-beat spies reported the new developments to The Beast.

"Curses!" roared The Beast when it heard the news.
"I'm losing control fast."

Consequently, it blasted forth a new command to the Dead-beats:
"Amass all the Dead-beat troops for battle.
We'll rattle their poise with unprecedented noise!"

Scrambling to escape The Beast's ire, the Dead-beats really just wanted to retire.

"We already know the end of the tale," mumbled a nameless Dead-beat.
"The negative always ends in prophetic defeat."

~ ~ ~

Meanwhile, back at *The Whole*, **R** extolled "confession" as good for the soul.

"Hate was accusing **d** while speaking through me. I was a decoy!" confessed **R**.

"what?" thought **d**. "i thought they hated me."

"Hate was using us, and we didn't even know it," professed **Q** with shame.

"is this a game?" wondered **d**. "who lives to forgive?"

"But Hate can't keep abusing by accusing if we catch it in the act," reasoned **N**.

"I hope **d** will live, and forgive us," said **U**.

"Now, without fuss, let's get back to reviving **d**."

So, back to work they went,
lovingly expelling each "de" word that had been
depressing, oppressing, suppressing, and dividing them
for such a long, long time.

The negative "de" words were put into a box, which was then locked,
and marked with a label that read:

~ **DESTRUCTIVE WORDS** ~
HAZARDOUS TO YOUR HEALTH

"Whew," said **R**, beginning to relax. "Love acts. I'm feeling better already."

"what is love?" questioned **d**. "i can even feel its effects on me."

"Thank you for your good work from the heart," concluded **h**.
"I'll stay here with **d** as you all now depart."

Affected by their sincere affection, **d** quietly reviewed his past.

"everything they said is true," thought **d**.
"i am so ashamed. i Deserve to be blamed.

"i have made compliance with Defiance into an art and a science.

"i am unworthy. my addiction to pleasure
has brought pain without measure.
my choices have led to a Dead end; but if you're listening, Be,
please . . . please . . . RSVP."

And with that sincere request, Be, always present and kind,
bestowed the gentle reminder,
"You are divine, embraced, and so very beloved.
Be glad evermore; you are good to the core."

"how can this be?" marveled **d**, having sensed Be's enveloping presence.

But that was it; he heard no more.

Undiscouraged, he vowed,"i must make a u-turn.
i will spurn the past, retract, amend, and learn what it means to be a real friend."

"first, i'll go to **O** and **K** and learn good words.
second, i'll begin to reveal their alpha-beat origin.
third, i'll say 'thank you, Be, for this whole new view,
is there anything special i can now Do for You?'"

With his sincere decision to amend,
d opened his eyes, surprised to see his "friend,"
h, praying quietly by his side.

"i'm so sorry, **h**, for all the bad that i've Done," cried **d**, squeezing **h**'s hand.
"please forgive me for instituting 'choice,' and negating your voice,
and the Deep freeze, and . . . "
beginning to sob, "and for continually kicking your poor, knobby knees."

"Please, please, have no fear," said **h**, wiping away **d**'s tear.
"All of us here have made mistakes hobbling along the wrong road.
But, knowing our true identity will lighten that load.

"The understanding that you are Be's will open your way
to a healthy and wealthy, revitalized day.

"Now, let's just be still until we feel filled up."

Within that humble quietude,
h exuded such love for **d** that their fear of past hurts
and all future harm
was unilaterally,
unquestionably, and undeniably disarmed.

"I forgive you, **d**; we're brothers, we're kin,
and there's no more future for bad or for sin.
We're secure as can be, because, you see,
we're each a part of Be's all-inclusive whole."

Thus, with this fraternal clarity of soul,
h was transformed into his original, capital role.

Overwhelmed with humility, **d** fell on his knees, whispering, "i want to be Be's."

"Then seize the opportunity and listen to Be," encouraged **H**.

"no, no, no, i'm not ready for Be. can we go see **O** and **K**?"

"Ok," agreed **H**, radiating the ambience of Soul, as he and **d**
emerged from *The Gathering Whole*.

Chapter 47

RECALIBRATION   **Frozen**

At Deadquarters, Fear and The Beast met to set up the date for the big downfall.

"I must attack those Beta-beats soon," roared The Beast with thunderous clamor,
as it hammered the floor with its tail.

Flailing about, Fear tried to calm its faltering nerve.

"How can I best serve?" asked Fear, trying to hide its abiding fear of failure.

Appearing not to notice, The Beast commanded,
"Listen here, Fear. Your mission is to smear their confidence with drear."

"What's 'drear'?" asked Fear, shivering with fright.

"It's a dripping, mental drizzle that dulls and depresses," growled the brute.

"Poison, you mean?" gulped Fear, having gathered that notion.

"Yes, poison remains my number-one potion," smiled The Beast, with a tinge of devotion.

"How does it work?" asked Fear, admitting under his breath, "I'm scared to death of poison."

"As they focus on the melancholy mix, they'll be transfixed with terror and dread.
Their fear will enlist the mist, which titillates and feeds the Beastly me."

"Oh, I see," murmured Fear uncomfortably. "And then?"

"I will feast on their demise," blubbered The Beast, with blood in his eyes.

"Yes, and then . . . ," hesitated Fear, fearing the worst.

"We'll attack with surprise at the rise of the mist.
Then, we'll twist and torment them all to death
with the life-zapping heat from my venomous breath."

"And Be?" whispered Fear.

"Bereft, Be will have nothing left."

"Will Being then disappear?" asked Fear.

"That's right," cackled The Beast with delight. "There'll be nothing here."

"And . . . and . . . what about me?" asked Fear.

"No need to worry; your reward is drawing near."

"Oh, oh dear," thought Fear, "that's what I've been afraid of."

"Now, beat it," bellowed The Beast. "It's time for my feast."

~ ~ ~

("Maybe I can slip in here," thought Fear, approaching *The Gathering Whole*.)

"So you want a new view?" asked **O**, who had invited **d** to meet for a "think" at *The Whole*.

"yes!" he affirmed. "i want to escape from the imprisoning pen that i put myself in."

"Sounds like you're open for Be'sness," replied Good-Works **O**.

"i am, but . . . "

("But you're afraid," suggested Fear, whispering right in **d**'s ear.)

"'But' . . . what?" asked **O**.

"well . . . well . . . " stammered **d**. "would you please lend me an 'o' so i can 'o'pen the pen that i've put myself in? i want out."

"Your desire, **d**, is the key," whispered **O**, with a wink to **K** standing at his side.

"well then, i'm as open as i can be," replied **d**.

("Oh dear," murmured Fear.)

"That's good, **d**. Before we begin, may I suggest that you capitalize the first letter of each sentence?" said **K**.

"oh, i don't think i'm worthy of that," whispered **d**, looking dejected.

"Yes, you are," encouraged **K**, as **d** looked up with surprise and hope in his eyes. "You have already passed the first test of humility, which will ensure your success."

"well then, what should my first capitalized sentence be?" pondered **d**. "oh, i know."

"Yes?" questioned **O**.

"Being is beautiful!" shouted **d**.

And **O** and **K** cheerfully agreed!

"Well then," said **K**, "let's proceed to the
Rehabilitation Station, where the Reign of Re's
uncovers, rejects, reverses, and
replaces each error with Truth."

"What do i have to do?" asked **d** with a tear,
feeling the shame of his destructive career.

"If you do the trusting, Truth will do the adjusting," advised **K**.
"And please, capitalize your I."

"I'll try," replied **d**, as the *reign*drops of reforming "re" words began to shower him with:

rethink, reverse, reject, renounce, remove, replace, repair, reevaluate, realign, revitalize, reclaim, revisit, recharge, renew, return, rebuild, resolve, restore, recuperate, remake, rebound, recoup, rejoice, rebirth, retell.

"This feels swell," sighed **d**.
"I feel brand new."

(Well, I can't get in here. Now what will I do?" ruminated Fear.)

They worked to redress
resentment, recrimination, and remorse,
until **d** agreed to capitalize every "I" —
when referring to himself.

And just as expected,
as **d** trusted, Truth adjusted.

Feeling the good effects, **d** said, "I want to be obedient."

"Then never be an 'I do later,'" warned **K**.

"What's that?" asked **d**.

"An 'I do later' does later what should be done now," explained **O**.

"When Be inspires, don't retire," warned **K**. "Do the work at once."

"I feel inspired to go for a walk," responded **d**.

"Then go," encouraged **O**.

~ ~ ~

With Fear bringing up the rear,
d walked and thought, and thought and walked,
until, finding himself in an unfamiliar neighborhood,
he beheld the frozen statue of little **k**.

"What's that?" he wondered.

("Maybe this is my chance," said Fear.)

Just then, Coach **K** rounded the corner.

("Oh dear," moaned Fear. "No way, not **K**.")

"Hey, **K**," greeted **d**. "What's that?" he asked, pointing to the frozen statue.

"The replacement **k**," she answered, aware that **d** had been absolved from his devilish past.

Staring in disbelief, he asked at last, "What happened? She looks demented."

"She was frightened and angered back in the day."

"By what?"

"By you, **d**," said **K**, with lovingkindness in her voice.

("And now he's mine," thought Fear.)

"I did that?" asked **d**, exuding sincere regret.

"No. Not you. It was malice <u>using</u> you," explained **K**.

"What's malice, and what does it do?"

"Malice is an unloving thought that cuts you in two."

"How do you get rid of it?" asked **d**.

"There's only one way."

"What's that?"

"Love."

"Of course," agreed **d**. "I have felt love's effect on me."

("Oh geez. Now I'm done," sighed Fear.
"There's no way to edge my wedge in here.")

"Yes, and now you can redeem the past and free frozen **k** at last," suggested **K**.

"Let's redeem her past today," said **d** with resolve,
"and mine, too."

"What a good thing to do," replied Coach **K**. "Why don't you sing her a song?"

"I'd like to," confessed **d**, "but I don't know how to sing."

"Have NO fear. Just be sincere," encouraged **K**.
"The know-how will flow out from inside of you."

"Really?" asked **d**.

"It's true; just listen," concluded **K**. "There's nothing here that can get in your way."

("I'm afraid this has not been a good day," fretted the exiting Fear.
"Love is negating the state we revere, so I'd better disappear
before the love felt here melts me all together.")

Then, getting really still,
d listened until a melody
began spilling into his singing heart.

Then opening up (and, quite frankly, giving him a start),
this song began expressing his healing essence in art.

"Lonely **k**, frozen all alone.
Lovely **k**, leave that rigid zone.
Fearful **k**, scared to death of something that went wrong.
Hopeful **k**, dismiss that tale; replace it with a song."

Touched by **d**'s song,
most of the Beta-beat came to sing along.

200

They voluntarily returned to the former scene of the "crime,"
grateful their future had been redeemed from the terror of Time.

Acknowledging their presence, **d** continued singing.

"Responsive **k**, listen for Be's voice.
Warm-hearted **k**, 'chilled' is not a choice.
Beloved **k**, you're not angry, sullen, gaunt.
Triumphant **k**, you own all the good you want."

Then, **J** arrived.

"Say, **d**, I have a thought," said **J**, caught up in the import of this moment. "May I sing?"

"Of course, **J**," sang **d**.
"Sing away."

"Listen, **k**," rapped **J** with a wink, tapping his feet.
"It's counted in four with a hefty upbeat:

1 . . . 2 . . . 3 . . . We're:
Not made up of fetters, lower letters, lines, or jots. They don't
Matter, never have; they can't hold you in this spot. You're not sus-
picious, repetitious; you're not living in a rut. And there's
Never been a flap, a snap, a freezer, or a cut."

"That's a wrap," sang **d**. "Let's all clap along."

"Listen, **k**. We're:
Not made up of fetters, lower letters, lines, or jots. They don't
Matter, never have; they can't hold you in this spot. You're not sus-
picious, repetitious; you're not living in a rut. And there's
Never been a flap, a snap, a freezer, or a cut."

Well, singing all together was such a joyful act,
they forgot about **k** until they heard an apocalyptic crack.

Looking back with surprise,
they turned 'round to see the transfigured **k** rising
like a phoenix from the ashes of her fiery past.

Aghast, they dashed to her, then knelt in respect to Be.

201

"Golly," whispered **G** in awe to **J**
(who smiled through his tears,
but had no words to say).

When **k**'s former hardened outline had ceased molting and melting,
the newly transparent Capital **K** began belting Be's signature song,

"There's no Be'sness like Soul Be'sness."

The letters were frozen with surprise,
because **K** was one of the Capitalized guys.
But by the time her singing was done,
a standing ovation had begun.

"Thanks for your acclamation," sang **K**, now defrosted and free.
"I've always known this day of defrost would become reality."

"**K**, please forgive me," pleaded **d**.

"I do, **d**; you're free.
You can relax; I know the facts."

Gazing about, **K** asked,
"Where's **j**? I must apologize for the unkind words I said about his jot.
It bothered me a lot,
until I realized that it had never been my thought."

"Here I am, **K**," smiled **J**.

"Where's your jot?" she asked. "You've lost it."

"And a lot of other 'nots,'" laughed **J**.
"But now, all is well. It's so good to see you, **K**."

"Likewise, **J**."

"Breaking a spell is easy now," sang **E**; "all we have to do is agree to agree."

"With Be," added Coach **K**.

"Forsooth," sang **Y**.
"Agree with Truth."

That simply stated Statement of Being captivated them all.

Finally, **d** broke the silence by asking,
"**K**, what is that 'Soul Be'sness' lyric you like to sing?
It has a familiar ring."

K replied with tears in her eyes.

"That song is my guardian ember.
I can't remember when it first nourished me,
but I know it has flourished in my heart since my embryonic start.
And whether I seem cut off, frozen, or hot,
I know its fervor will never ever stop.

"You see, its radiating beam has continued to sing in me,
even though, to you, I seemed to be irreversibly broken in two."

"Beautiful," wept Coach **K**. "Patience has rewarded you."

"That was Be singing to you with steadfast quietude," sang **Q**.

"Will you teach us Be's song?" asked Coach **K**, already humming along.

"Sure," sang **K**, in a voice pure and true.

"Excuse me," asked **W**. "Before we sing, may I ask a question?"

"Of course," answered **K**.

"I'm writing a book that links *freedom* with *friendship*.
Can you give me some words of wisdom to include?"

"Well," replied **K** thoughtfully,
"let's be warm to each other and not cold.
Let's learn not to spurn.
Let's live and forgive;
and together, let's express the love that's within us, around, and above."

"Brilliant," sang **W**, recording every word. "Anything else?"

"Yes," confessed **d** with unaccustomed serenity.
"It's time that you all know about our true origin and identity."

"Please continue," asked **I**, at his side to lend support.

"When I imagined you in physical form, declaring you as the Beta-beat norm,
I purposely concealed from you the fact that you were Be's Alpha-beat creation,
existing untouched from the physicality of my imagination."

"Are you saying that our true nature is physique-free?" asked **Z**.

"Yes; as Be's Alpha-beat, your anatomy is a mental body of thought,"
explained **d**. "It is completely physique-free."

"Why did you deceive us?" asked **I**, remembering his own transformation from **i** to **I**.

"I was angry because I had knees and you didn't,"explained **d**.
"I wanted you to serve the Death-Wish Cartel just like me."

"Thank you, **d**," replied **T** tenderly, "for telling us the truth.
But you know, dear one, it takes two to make a goof."

"That's right," agreed **Y**. "We must take responsibility for being deceived."

"If I hadn't believed you, **d**, none of this would have happened," confessed **E**.

"That's right, **E**," affirmed Coach **K**.
"Thank you, **d**, for reconnecting us with our true individuality."

"We're Be's Alpha-beats from now on," shouted **E**. "Do you all agree?"

"Won't you join me in shouting, 'Yes!'" bellowed **S**.

Much to **d**'s amazement,
they all began to holler with joyful solidarity.

Enjoying the singularity of thought, Coach **K** capped the happy occasion with,
"Let's always make good choices that fuel our voices,
and sing **K**'s song again."

Happily, they all joined with **K** and Coach **K** in singing another rousing chorus of
"There's no Be'sness like Soul Be'sness."

Chapter 48

ELIMINATION

Fear Not

Observing this unfolding Alpha-beat exposé,
the deflated Dead-beats found they had little to say.

"This whole state of Un is becoming undone," droned one Dead-beat to another. "It's all a lie."

"When the Alpha-beat is unified, we'll be mortified."

"Demystified."

"Should we inform The Beast about this revitalized **K**?"

"Nay — no way!"

"I predict The Beast will soon be called 'the late, great Hate.'"

"A fitting fate."

Straight off, The Beast came into view.

"I need to feast," shouted the Beast impatiently. "Where's Fear?"

"Oh dear," sighed Fear, fretting in its own mist.

"Fear, wherever you are, I insist you appear," commanded The Beast.

"I, I, I'm here," stammered Fear, instantly materializing.

"Where's the drear you said would appear?"

"I'm afraid it's not here," whispered Fear, cowering with shame in the shadow of The Beast.

"Why not?" screamed The Beast.

"I can't penetrate their mental atmosphere," whispered Fear.

"Why?" roared The Beast.

"Their love of Be is too powerful," cried Fear, clearly fearing its imminent demise.

"What?" shouted The Beast, as if mortally wounded.
"This love 'infection' must cease."

"I'm trying," wept Fear, as its self-imposed pressure increased.

"You're useless; it's time you pay the price!" screamed The Beast, grabbing Fear.
"I'm famished . . . and YOU
are on my menu."

"No, no," shrieked Fear, pleading,
"Please. Not now.
Not here!"

The ravenous Beast, salivating profusely,
lifted Fear into his gargantuan mouth, roaring, "You, Fear, are going south!"

The Beast chewed Fear and each of its falsities
up into a putrid, pulverized pulp,
which the brute swallowed down with a gross, gargantuan gulp.

As the Dead-beats waited with bated breath,
they swore they heard Fear imploring,
"Hate!
Pleeease regurgitate."

"Burrrrrrrrpppppppp!" belched the despised, super-sized Beast with glee,
signifying the finale of its feast, and the fatal downfall and demise of Fear.

Then, with a mocking air, it sarcastically declared,
"Oh dear . . . I fear . . . our feast . . . of Fear . . . was a waste."

"How did it taste?" asked a brave Dead-beat.

"Sweet on the lips, but sour in the gut," glowered the gluttonous gourmand.

"What now?" asked a sycophant Dead-beat.

"Now," snarled the satiated Beast,
"the hour has come in Un,
for this war of confusion at last be to won!"

Adjustments

Meanwhile, **d** returned to the Rehabilitation Station with Good-Works **O** and Coach **K**.

"Would you like to commune with Be about what happened today?" suggested Coach **K**.

"Be, as in Being?" asked **d**, with trepidation.

"Yes."

"Oh no; I am not good enough to commune with Be," sighed **d**.

"Don't you think that Be already knows your wishes and desires?" asked **O**.

"I suppose so; Be knows everything," replied **d**.

"Be knows that goodness fills all space,
so there is no place for *bad* or *disgrace*," confirmed Coach **K**.

Humbly gazing up at **K**'s kind face, **d** asked, "What do you think I should I do?"

"Trust Be, dear **d**, and Truth will adjust," replied **K**. "Now you need to be still."

Filling up with emotion, **d** looked at **O** for approval.

"Just trust Be, and Truth will adjust,"
whispered the big-hearted **O**, summoning Silence to assist.

Being obedient, **d** found a quiet alcove and sat down at last to ponder his squandered past.

Closing his eyes, he sank deeper and deeper
into the tender tranquility of Silence,
welcoming the clarity of Be's unseen, cleaning cleanser.

This purification dissolved any residue of fear
and inspired uplifting thoughts to bud and appear.

As he felt his original heart being restored,
he simply began to trust Be more.

"Be, how does one correct bad vision?" asked **d**
sincerely from the core of his adoring new heart.

And Be replied silently,
"Being is seeing with singular precision.
Being is achieving anything our mind can envision.

"Being is your open door to freedom and bliss.
Being, you could say, is my universal kiss."

Be continued speaking soundlessly to **d**'s receptive heart,
"You'll soon understand that, wherever you are, I've been there before,
and regardless of how much I've given, I'll still give you more."

Then, to end, Be whispered like a soft, summer breeze,
"Precious one, Life is Being, and Being is ease."

"Life is Being?" thought **d**. "So, dying is a lie about Life.
No wonder Evil was afraid the belief in death would die."

Energized by this higher understanding,
d continued to contemplate Be as pure Being.

"Well then, dear Be, if Life is Being, then how should I live?"

"Living is giving, and receiving in return."

Then, more thoughtfully, **d** asked, "And what should I think?"

"You're thinking when you are thanking me," answered Be.

"Oh, thank You, Be, for all the good that You see."

The questions and answers continued to enlighten,
until the understanding of eternal Truth slowly dawned upon **d**,
and this grand conclusion crystallized into certain clarity.

"Being *is* . . . is!"

Understanding the profound simplicity and inevitability of Life,
d declared emphatically, "This is the fact! There is <u>no</u> lack, because Being is Be's Be'sness."

Grasping that actuality, **d** pondered what it means "to be"
for what seemed like an eternity,
and that epoch workout empowered him to determine Time's fate.

Consequently, dear reader, on that auspicious date,
at that very moment, the curse called
time
was positively reversed and sentenced to
emit
effortless beams of delight — forever.

Impressed that Time was a nonentity,
d implored, with respect, from every pore of his being,
"Be, tell me, please, about You.
I want to know You the way You know me."

Be smiled at that heartfelt request, but felt it best to focus on the original **D**.

"Wisdom," sang Be, "is pure harmony.

"You've never been lost, or absent, or bad.
How could my likeness be a cad, sad, or mad?

"Oh no, precious one, you're a voice in my choir,
Created to sing, composed to inspire.

"So sing your unique song. Don't ever lament,
For your perfect conception is the only event.

"Waste not a moment regretting the past,
For our likeness is constant and ever stands fast."

"You mean, I'm just like You?" asked **d** incredulously.

"You and I are one and the same,
Homogenous, identical, and lit as one flame.

"Harmonious, single, we're both the same kind,
Living and loving at home in my Mind.

209

"*And* what's mine has always been, and always will be, yours."

"Well then, if I want to be like You,
shouldn't I agree with You and Your singular view
of Me?" sang **d**.

"Indubitably," sang Be.

So, **d** turned his question into a statement,
and began declaring it with sincerity, clarity, and conviction.

"I am just like Be. I am good, like Be. I am the mirror image of Be."

"That's the true view," sang Be. "And what do you have?"

"I have what is Yours.
I can only have what You have.
If You don't have it, neither do I."

"That's right. And why?"

"Because I have always been just like You."

"Since when?

"Since . . . "

As the full Truth unfolded to **d**, he paused with awe.

"Yes?" sang Be, inviting a response.

"Forever," sang **d**.
"Forever and ever, and ever and ever,
and ever and ever, forever . . . together!!"

Suddenly, **d** remembered Time's grasping hands, and, gasping, he cried,
"There is no 'was' or 'will be' in reality.
Time never, ever touched me, because all life exists in Be.

"Time isn't real because it was 'then,'
and 'then' isn't 'now,' and so it couldn't have been;
and it never will be — because *now* is Be's Be'sness.

210

"Wow! I get it," cried **d**. "Good never begins or ends; it just — is.

"But . . . how do I remain in Eternity?" pondered **d**,
pioneering the domain of a new understanding.

"I don't ever want to fall away — not even for a day," he confessed.

Humbling himself before Be, **d** bowed on his knees, whispering,
"Please tell me, Be: what is the key to living in Eternity?"

And he waited and waited . . .
primed to receive the sublime
Key to Being.

Finally, ever so gently, Be sang,
"There is no 'But' in your divine pedigree."

Instantly, an inaudible, *a cappella* choir,
harmonizing,
rising higher and higher
in beauty and soul,
serenaded Be
and the beloved idea, **D**.
With rhapsodic song, the whole-hearted throng
agreed unanimously that one and all belong to Be.

"Oh, I see," sang **d**, as the choir silently hummed along.
"There is no exception to your perfect conception.
And I am so grateful for that which IS and for that which IS not."

Thus, being in perfect agreement with Be,
Capital **D** was instantaneously freed.

Exuding wonder from the hub of his core,
D rubbed his eyes, singing, "I want to know more!"

Well, as you can imagine, the choir clapped its hands,
and Be blew a kiss
in this swelling Niagara of polyphonic bliss.

(However, it would be remiss
not to reveal that the sheen of this euphoric scene
was unseen in the bland Land of Un.)

Feeling this unseen but inspired glee,
D sang in the very same key,
"I know I am Your Capital **D**.
And Be, I just love Being me."

"Yippee!" sang Be.

Thus, Be and **D** rejoiced in that moment wed like a husband and wife,
communing in their pure, undefiled Language of Life.

In true bliss, **D** whispered,
"Now that I know I can trust You, Be, I am satisfied.
You have given me more than enough."

And this attitude of gratitude really pleased Be.

Being completely at ease, **D** sang,
"Please, dearest Be, is there anything special I can now do for You?"

"Smile," beamed Be with brilliant delight.
And **D** smiled back, vanquishing the night.

~ ~ ~

When the letters discerned that **D** had recapitalized, there was some concern.

"What if he's that old, obnoxious **D** who still wants to do dastardly deeds?" remarked **Q** to **P**.

"Well," declared **P**, "I'll just go and see **D** for myself."

Upon returning, **P** reported, "**D** looks absolutely beatific."

"That's terrific!" exclaimed **Q**.

"Wait till you see him!" laughed **P**. "He's a pile of smiles!"

P then proceeded to inform the Alpha-beat of **D**'s complete transformation.

So naturally, **Y** and **Z** threw a party,
and they did it up right.
All in all, it was a picture-perfect sight.

They serenaded **D** with an Ode to Being composed by Good-Works **O**.
Then, **P** recited poetry and **CO** put on a show.

So happy that the lie called "past" had passed away,
all the letters hoped this celebratory blast would last.

"What's next?" asked **X** of **Z**.

"Let's have a parade!"

Just then, the light that inspired the celebratory parade faded,
as a terrifying, tornadic twister whistled, thundered and raged across Dim.

Chapter 50

War!

DECIMATION

"Forget the parade. It's time to invade," thundered the devilish Beast,
as its airborne Dead-beat Divisions
filled the sky with legions of mosquito-like munitions.
"The War of Nerves has begun!"

"No nerve can invade our verve," shouted the original **O**.
"This invasion will test our mettle,
but we won't settle
for less than perfection."

"Take your stations for outgoing irritations," countermanded The Beast,
marshaling its troops.

"Now, zoom in and lower the boom!
Don't forget, our goal is the tomb!"

It seemed to the Alpha-beat that a curtain of gray fog was descending,
covering them all with a mental mist and a foggy haze
that wreaked of havoc and smelled like malaise.

"Don't avert your gaze," commanded Coach **K**. "This is the beginning of the end of their
show, so hold fast to everything good that you know."

"The mist is designed to neutralize our will to resist," shouted **I**.
"Remember, this is too bad to be true. With every showdown, we will show *up*!"

With legions of Dead-beats buzzing and beating their wings, eager to torment with
accusations, the brutal Beast heartlessly charged the Alpha-beat as:

GUILTY

of the following crimes:
1. The reversal of Time,

2. The eradication of Hate,

3. The intimidation of Fear,

and

4. The upheaval of Evil.

"Guard your thoughts," yelled **I**, as the Beast's deadly, deforming divisions began attacking
simultaneously on two fronts.

"Divide them," shouted The Beast to its platoon of outer Dead-beats.
"Keep beating their backs with complaints till they crack."

Then, Coach **K** commanded above the uproar,
"Don't be afraid. Just love even more."

"Huddle together," called **H**. "This attack lacks Soul."

214

"Think 'whole,'" shouted **W**, as the deafening noise increased.

"Love is the only weapon that will win," shouted **U** in the center of the pack.
"It will sack The Beast and its attacking Dead-beats."

The letters piled into a pyramid to hide **D** from The Beast,
and as long as they huddled, their peace didn't cease.

The Beast's repugnant stench debased the whole space,
making it hard to love such a malevolent face.
Frantically, it slobbered commands and ridiculous demands.

"Inner Dead-beats, paralyze with infected fables and lies," roared The Beast.

Accordingly, hoards of Dead-beats fluttered with fury,
hurling licentious lexicons of violent invectives at the letters.

"The goal is to extinguish their Alpha-beat soul," screamed The Beast.
"I must maintain my beastly control."

But the letters held on,
marshaling monumental magnitudes of grace,
until **D** implored from the depth of his core,
"Arise and maintain high beams.
This is Be's battle; disregard beastly schemes.

"There is no destructive power or need to cower,
We must refuse to conjugate,
cooperate, or participate
with any destructive Dead-beat verb."

"Now I'm really perturbed,"
shouted The Beast, with smoke and steam billowing out of its ears.
Realizing that **D** had become the leader of the opposition, it screamed,
"Give me **D**, or you all will die."

"You're just a big lie," they cried. We will not be denied our victory."

So, beam they did to **D** and each other,
while their trust in Being fortified them like a babe with its mother.

Be sang in each heart, which strengthened their nerve
and nourished their thoughts with the desire to serve.

They acknowledged Be's supremacy right there in the fight,
accepting nothing but goodness with all of their might.

And this increased poise
deflected The Beast's poisonous noise.

As the battle continued to rage and ravage, the desperate Beast summoned aid
from its
arsenal of negativity,
so that:

Dread confused,
Lust bruised,
Anger belched,
Pride squelched.

Shame blamed,
Scorn maimed,
Sorrow cried,
and
Addiction lied.

The Dead-beats were deadly and vicious,
but they were destroying only what was wicked and malicious.

In other words, they were killing themselves.

"Wrong is yielding to right's shield," shouted **Q**, as **U** began singing,
"Love's alive, Love's alive,"
knowing down deep that they all would survive.

Meanwhile,
the Death-Wish Curse and the Capitals' unison verse
continued to battle on all fronts.

Although The Beast's sting stung all those protecting **D**,
its infecting sting had no effect on the Alpha-beat singers,
whose concordant chant was evolving into pure tones of love.

Shocked that the letters would unselfishly protect the very **D** that had deformed and distorted their identity, the enraged Beast bellowed, "Who is like me?"

"We are like Be," sang the Capital letters in unison.

As the Dead-beat noise increased, The Beast shrieked,
"I, The Beast, don't like that answer. I repeat, who is like me?"

They sang even louder, "We are like Be!"

"If you won't surrender **D** to me, I will kill you," screamed the Beast.

> The Dead-beats tried to comply,
> but they didn't think or even ask, "why?"
> They were fabricated to imitate,
> and that's just what they did.

"If you won't surrender **D** to me, I will kill you," screamed the Dead-beats.

"Who is like me?" screamed The Beast, irritated by his own Dead-beats.

"Who is like me?" repeated The Beast's army of imitators.

> Mimicked by its own minions, The Beast, in its craving to be revered, went crazy!

"Worship Me, The Beast," it demanded.

The buzzing Dead-beats, void of all understanding, repeated, "Worship me, The Beast."

Bloated with rage, engaged by its own Dead-beats, The Beast screamed, "Serve Me!"

The Dead-beats echoed, "Serve Me!"

The Beast screamed, "No, stupid, Me!"

They echoed, "No, stupid, Me!"

In a fury now, The Beast's shouting amplified: "ME!"

Followed by the Dead-beats', "ME!"

Then, "ME!!"

"ME!!"

"ME!!!"

"ME!!!"

"NO! ME!!!!"

"NO! ME!!!!" the Dead-beats repeated in a maddening drone devoid of all tone.

The more "Me's" said, the redder The Beast got, until giggles,
then chuckles from the Alpha-beat wriggled
into uproarious laughter.

It was a humorous sight to see The Beast losing its might.

"This Beastly buffoon is a funny cartoon," shouted **E** to **R**, laughing heartily.

"Curses!" screamed The Beast, stinging everything in sight,
including its own Dead-beats.
"Unity is negating my attack."

But The Beast kept pelting the letters with noxious nega-tudes,
expecting their Be-attitudes of gratitude to crack.

"I hate Be!" screamed The Beast insanely.

The Dead-beats echoed, "I hate Be. I hate Be," with inane simulation.

"Hate!" shouted The Beast.

"Hate!" echoed the Dead-beats.

On and on raged their litany of death,
designed to kill with each intoxicated breath.

In the Alpha-beat huddle, **F** whispered, "I thought The Beast hated us."

"We're nothing to The Beast," responded **G**, "because The Beast is nothing."

"It's just a big, old, bad belief," affirmed **C**.

"It's nothing unless we believe it," added **X**. "Now that we see its disguise, we won't be fooled by any more lies.

"Its only hope for survival is **D**, so keep on loving. Persistence is the key."

"I feel loved," thought **D** with tears in his eyes. "I feel Be's love in me, and gee, I really love these guys."

Just then, The Beast zeroed in for a final attack, while each letter, embracing **D**, counteracted by loving right back.

Love's circulation inspired such
concentration that
thought-seeds
began
to sprout,
then bud,
and blossom
within the soil of their
collective understanding,
forming a cohesive mental bond.
This solid commitment, rooted in love, inspired an enormous explosion
of consciousness, releasing a brilliance that shielded them all from The Beast.

Instantly, the Alpha-beat letters knew that
confusion
had been defused
by the fusion
called
Love.

This beatific moment of devotion accordingly inspired a surge of emotion.

"**D** is weeping," called **H** from the bottom of the pile.

"Comfort him," yelled **C** as the behemoth Beast hovered, covering all with its frigid air and the darkest shadow yet.

219

Stunned by the darkness, **D** cried in a momentary lapse,
"Look what I've done.
They're all going to die because of me. This just cannot be.
Stop," he shouted to The Beast. "Stop! Spare them! Take me."

But with all the noise, the screaming Beast didn't hear **D**'s plea.

It was a good thing, for the befouled Beast began inflating
with hatred at an unbelievable rate.

"Gee!" cried **G**, "The Beast is burgeoning!" as its massive corpulence towered over
the Alpha-beat, the Dead-beats, and the entire battlefield.

With its venomous, harpoon-like tail flailing in a frenzy,
the putrid barbs of The Beast's poisonous premise
punctured its distended abdomen with a
"pop,"

d e f l a t i n g

all menace and malice

with a simple . . .

whimpered . . .

. . .

pfffft.

The Caps were shocked, and dumbfounded, too,
that The Beast had *vanished* without residue.

Lacking its leader, the attack was sacked —
(and that hellacious cartel with its Beast never *ever* came back.)

"It's gone. There's nothing left," exclaimed **X** in awe.

"We've been afraid of a gutless Beast!" shouted **F**.

"It really was *nothing*," nodded **N**.

"Why did we fall for that delusion?" wondered **J** to the speechless crew.

"We were confused," offered **Q** in a quandary.

"And misled," added **W**.

"Thick-headed and gullible," whispered **J**.

"Hey," yelled **U**, breaking the spell. "Here's our proof.
Love can make even The Beast go poof."

"Where are the Dead-beats?" asked **A**.

"Gone with zee Beast," answered **Z**.

"They existed only in the Beast's imagination," explained Coach **K**, "and ours."

"Well, this has turned out to be a zippity-dazzling good day," winked **A** to **Z**,
who agreed, saying, "Yup, but we'd better get up and off of **D**."

Chapter 51

VINDICATION

Embraced

So, they happily climbed off of each other tremulous with anticipation, but
their joy was dashed by the sight of **D** lying motionless at the bottom of the heap.

"**D** looks deceased!" cried **C**.

"We must see the original **D**," expressed **X**, unimpressed.

Even though **D** looked deceased, he was actually feeling great inner peace.

"I know there's no death or strife in life," thought **D**,
aware that the others were caring for him by declaring the truth.

"Being can't goof," affirmed **Z**.

"Or collapse," stated **T** with conviction.

"A limit, mishap, or relapse of good is impossible," belted out **K** in her trademark song.

K's belting vibrations were felt by **D**,
causing any last nugget of negativity to melt away.

Unaware that **D** was conscious, the others
persisted in their vindicating act through singing.

"Let's surround **D** with Be-Attitudes of gratitude and peace," sang **C**.

"I'll begin," sang **A**, "with ABUNDANCE."

"Ah," sighed **D**. "This is lovely."

"How about BELOVE**D** and CONFI**D**ENT," sang **B** and **C**.

"**D**EAR, EN**D**URING, FOUN**D**ED, AND GROUN**D**ED," sang **E**, **F**, and **G**.

"I really love **E**, **F**, **G**, and, of course, **A**, **B**, and **C**," thought **D**. "I'm regaining my foothold."

"HAR**D**Y, I**D**EAL, JOINE**D**, and KIN**D**," sang **H**, **I**, **J**, and **K**.

"LAU**D**ATORY, MO**D**EST, NEE**D**ED, OR**D**ERLY, and PROVE**D**,"
harmonized **L**, **M**, **N**, **O**, and **P**.

"This is moving!" thought **D**, with tears in his eyes.
"They're proving their love for Be by seeing the perfect image of me."

"QUALIFIE**D** and RA**D**IANT," sang **Q** and **R**.

"STEA**D**FAST," sang **S**, holding onto his tone.

"And TEN**D**ER," harmonized **T**, happy to not be singing alone.

"UN**D**ERSTAN**D**ING, VIN**D**ICATED, WON**D**ERFUL," chimed **U**, **V**, and **W** in one harmonious chord.

And so it went, with **X** adding, "X-ONERATE**D**" and **Y**, "YIEL**D**ING."

"And," sang **Z** with a flourish, "to end with a trump,
it is my pleasure to put **D** into **D**AZZLE, and put him up front!"

"Three cheers for **D**!" sang **P**.

D grinned through his tears with gratitude, thinking,
"Only love can translate jeers into cheers."

"Our **D**'s alive and surely will thrive," sang **U**, as softly as a lullaby.

Night fell as the Alpha-beat all sang along,
and the song filled **D** and the singers with serene satisfaction.

"I love you, Be, and know that you are right here with me," sang **D** with a sigh.

To which Be replied,
"Dear one, where else would I be and what else can I see?
To me, everyone always has been in my sweet . . . and complete . . .
brilliant Alpha-beat."

Having felt the kiss
of Be's celestial bliss,
each individual letter felt blessed
and divinely caressed.

And as they continued to sing, a wee beacon of light
glistened through **D**, christening the night.

"Look," whispered **I**. "It's Be's delight reflected by **D**!"

"What's delight?" whispered **W**.

"Be's pleasure without measure," smiled **A**.

"**D** is our delight, too," affirmed **H**.

"Love restores," affirmed **E**, gazing at **D** with the *élan* of eternal ease.

Now, for the first time in Un,
each Alpha-beating heart was harmonizing as *one*.

"**B**eing seems brighter tonight," observed **D**, opening his eyes with surprise
to see unconditional love beaming back at him through the Alpha-beat eyes.

Naturally receptive to the Alpha-beat might,
D arose be-knighted, reflecting his original delight.

As **D** claimed his true identity, the dawn of understanding lit up the sky,
while cascades of Truth answered every how, what, and why.

Gasping, **D** cried, "What breathtaking sights,"
as Be's effulgent creation unveiled splendiferous, new heights.

"Love is here to stay!" sang **D**, as the Alpha-beat enjoyed the light of that luminous night.

~ ~ ~

Dear reader, you may be wondering what Be had to say. Just this:

"Love is the rule, the principle, the way.
Today, you lived it and can honestly say,
'I <u>am</u> divine, embraced, and beloved,
because I <u>know</u> Being encircles all — both beneath and above.'

"Beloved, you have discovered the scientific fuel.
Simply live, work, and play by its rule.

"The jewel of satisfaction will be your precious prize.
Just listen, love, laugh, and be wise."

Chapter 52

UNIFICATION

Peace

With the extinction of The Beast/Hate, Fear, Evil, and Time,
the sublime air of independence
dispelled the cloudy curse, revealing Be's gleaming Capital City.

As royal and loyal citizens of the city, their native power,
insight, and abilities flowered.
They met daily at *The Gathering Whole*,
delighting in Be's gentle reign —
the peaceful reign of Soul.

They wanted to be just like Be,
so they requested a code of thinking
to keep them pure and free.

And to this Be agreed,
giving them *Be-do's* and *Be-don't's*,
to protect them from nega-tudes like
"I can't" and "we won't."

Such devotion to Being pleased Be no end,
because creator and creation were united as "friend."
Naturally, this atmosphere of freedom (as it always should)
empowered the letters to work unselfishly for their reciprocal good.

This led to self-government where Principle stood supreme,
and each letter was responsible
for rejecting any double-minded scheme.

The Alpha-beat developed systems of Be'sness, efficient and kind,
and the economy flourished with both demand and supply in mind.
Be's providence smiled on every neighborhood of good,
where all concepts progressed as they naturally should.

While **W** was writing her book about the freeing effect of friendship on letters,
M launched a search for other Alpha-beats, and perchance, other debtors.

With **D**'s return to the fold,
The Gathering Whole glittered like a garden of gold.
Their energy was synergy and focus was their fuel.
Living was easy and joy was the rule.

And wouldn't you know, with each evolving day,
all outlining fetters simply fell away.
For that's the way it was in the city that glistened,
the one that they christened

"Love."

~ ~~

Then, one day, **M**, mighty and fit,
returning from a long exploratory trip,
marched into the city with an unknown band
of letters from many a foreign Alpha-beat land.

The unknown configurations were keen,
but ones the Alpha-beat had never, ever seen.

They conversed with unfamiliar words
that sounded absurd, blurred — all previously unheard.

In response, the Alpha-beat letters were whistling, waving,
and welcoming the unknown Alpha-beat letters into their city with joy.

"Maybe this is a test," discerned **I** to **U**.

"Whatever! We'll just love as we usually do," smiled **U**.

Then **M** heralded, "Meet our neighbors in Be's Universe of Good."

And **C** shed happy tears as a selfless **C** would.

"Our Be is so awesome; the Be we adore has created these neighbors,
and infinitely more than we could have imagined before," announced **M**.

"This is radical," said **R**. "We're from the same root."

With all saluting that fact, the last fetter cracked, dissolving away.

"Where did our fetters go?" asked **W**.

"Don't know," replied **Y**. "Where do dreams go when we awake?"

"Dreams and fetters are fiction," responded **T**, trembling with glee.
"We're translating back into formless facts of actual Being."

"Yippee!" shouted **W** and **Y** in unison.

"Let's mingle and rejoice," exclaimed **Z** to each and every letter.

"How do you do, and what do you say?" sang **A** to her new neighbors.
"This day was made for a celebratory parade."

In response, Be's choir silently sang an *a cappella*, "Hooray!"

And wouldn't you know, that was the moment Be called from within their hearts,
"Come. Come Home to stay."

Intuitively, they knew just what to do and say,
welcoming the dawn of a new Scientific way — of Being.

"Wait, please," cried **W**.
"May I leave my book, in case any unknown letter should roam
and needs to know how to find its way home?"

"Double OK," agreed the **O**'s and **K**'s,
knowing that it would point out the way for any unknown fettered-letter
still soundly asleep in Un's unquestioning deep.

Then, all the original Capitals, along with **O** and **K**,
smiled in agreement, and with that unifying act, collectively took flight into The Bright.

Transported above the rising currents of immeasurable love,
each billed and cooed like an ascending dove
winging its way to the impeccable portal of
Be's peaceful Parapet of Light,
where existence is forever
and everything
is
all right.

Am Too!

Chapter 53

Emancipation

"Where am I?" asked **D**, as he awoke from his dream to see what had been the *unseen*.

Safely embraced in the sunshine of Soul, **D** realized,
"I have always been perfectly whole!"

Gazing about, **D** recognized Be's Golden Beach of Blue,
where Infinity's Ocean of Love hugs the Sky of Everything True.

"Tell me, **D**, what have you learned today?" asked Be
(like a parent whose child has just come home from school).

"Somewhere outside," replied **D**, "in a world that's untrue,
there may be a suffering dreamer who doesn't know what to do.
In that unreal scheme, it's begging for a clue,
and I'm yearning to tell that dreamer all about you."

"What would you tell that dreamer?" asked Be.

"Love will fix the dream."

"**D**, my dear delight, if you're seeking a dream mission,
I give you permission.
However, to avoid the need to think or act twice,
may I offer a brief word of advice?"

D nodded expectantly.

"Don't fix the dream," whispered Be with a wink.

"Wake the dreamer."

"Of course," smiled **D**, twinkling with inspiration.

"And now, my beloved Alpha-beat," sang Be,
"let's play and sing.

"You know you are always so beautiful to me."

And so, they all joined in another glorious chorus of
"There's no Be'sness like Soul Be'sness,"
and had a very good time —
eternally, that is.

~ ~ ~

However, faithful reader, lest you fear an unknown letter could appear,
remember that **W**'s book remained behind in Un,
lying open with this message of hope:

"Dear Friend,
When all seems forsaken,
and if you care to look,
you'll find that the key to freedom
resides in this little, open book."

~ ~ ~

And that's just what happened!

~ The End ~

I would like to acknowledge and thank:

The Source of All Being
that inspired this spiritual parable
in a moment of personal stillness during a nor'easter in March of 2001.

Charlotte de Lissovoy, who steadfastly mentored and lovingly challenged me
*from the beginning, when I brought her the first inspired pages of **B** in 2002.*

*Carol Niederbrach, Aunt **B**, whose final edits of the 2019 edition were penned*
with generosity of spirit, patience, perspicacity, and joyful professionalism.

John Richard Barth, my precious husband and best friend,
benefactor, counselor, editor and trusted companion.
His listening ear and discerning eye helped to clarify the story
and uplift it to its present form.

and

You, the readers, who have blessed these pages
with your kind attention and thoughtful response.

With love and gratitude,
Jessie Barth

Perry, NY
January 12, 2019

*Cover design by Rachel Richter of **Olive and Ink**, Perry, NY*

Perry Principle Press Logo designed by Tracy Rozanski, Perry, NY

Made in the USA
Monee, IL
24 October 2020